ESCAPE PLAN

- ① Decode the cryptic messages left by my mother.

- ② Run away.

- ③ Do not get caught.

- ④ Find my mother.

- ⑤ Choose my own destiny.

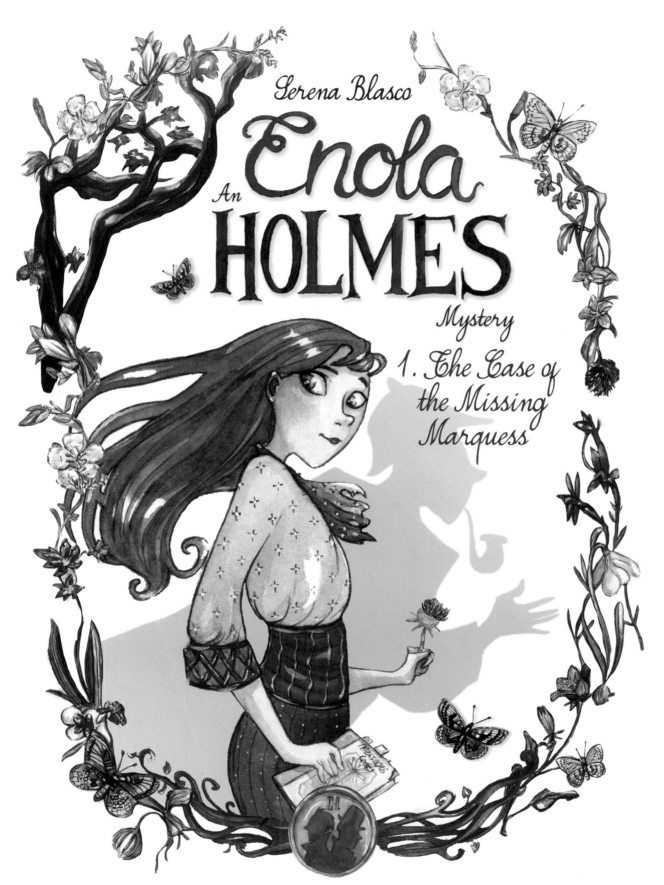

Serena Blasco

An Enola
HOLMES

Mystery

1. The Case of
the Missing
Marquess

Based on the novel by Nancy Springer

EURO COMICS
ENGLISH EDITION   GRAPHIC NOVELS

An imprint of IDW Publishing

I'd like to thank my family for their support and for being my first fans.

I'd also like to thank everyone from Studio Gottferdom, and our friends and colleagues, both near and far, for their precious advice and encouragement. I would list the names of all these individuals, but I would risk going on for too long (a little like the tags in clothing—in the end, it scratches and we end up cutting it!).

And also to all my other friends for having accompanied me, and for having followed my progress so closely.

— Serena Blasco

EuroComics.us

EDITOR Dean Mullaney • ART DIRECTOR Lorraine Turner
TRANSLATION Jeremy Melloul and Dean Mullaney

EuroComics is an imprint of IDW Publishing
a Division of Idea and Design Works, LLC
2765 Truxtun Road • San Diego, CA 92106
www.idwpublishing.com • EuroComics.us

IDW Publishing
Greg Goldstein, President and Publisher
John Barber, Editor-In-Chief
Robbie Robbins, EVP/Sr. Art Director
Cara Morrison, Chief Financial Officer
Matt Ruzicka, Chief Accounting Officer
Anita Frazier, SVP of Sales and Marketing
David Hedgecock, Associate Publisher
Jerry Bennington, VP of New Product Development
Lorelei Bunjes, VP of Digital Services
Justin Eisinger, Editorial Director, Graphic Novels & Collections
Eric Moss, Senior Director, Licensing and Business Development

Ted Adams, Founder and CEO of IDW Media Holdings

ISBN: 978-1-68405-336-0
First Printing, November 2018

Distributed to the book trade by Penguin Random House
Distributed to the comic book trade by Diamond Book Distributors

Based on the novel *The Case of the Missing Marquess*
— An Enola Holmes Mystery by Nancy Springer
copyright © 2006 by Nancy Springer

Graphic adaptation copyright © 2015 Jungle, by Serena Blasco
originally published in France as *La Double Disparition*

Special thanks to Flora Boffy-Prache of Steinkis Groupe, Justin Eisinger, and Alonzo Simon.

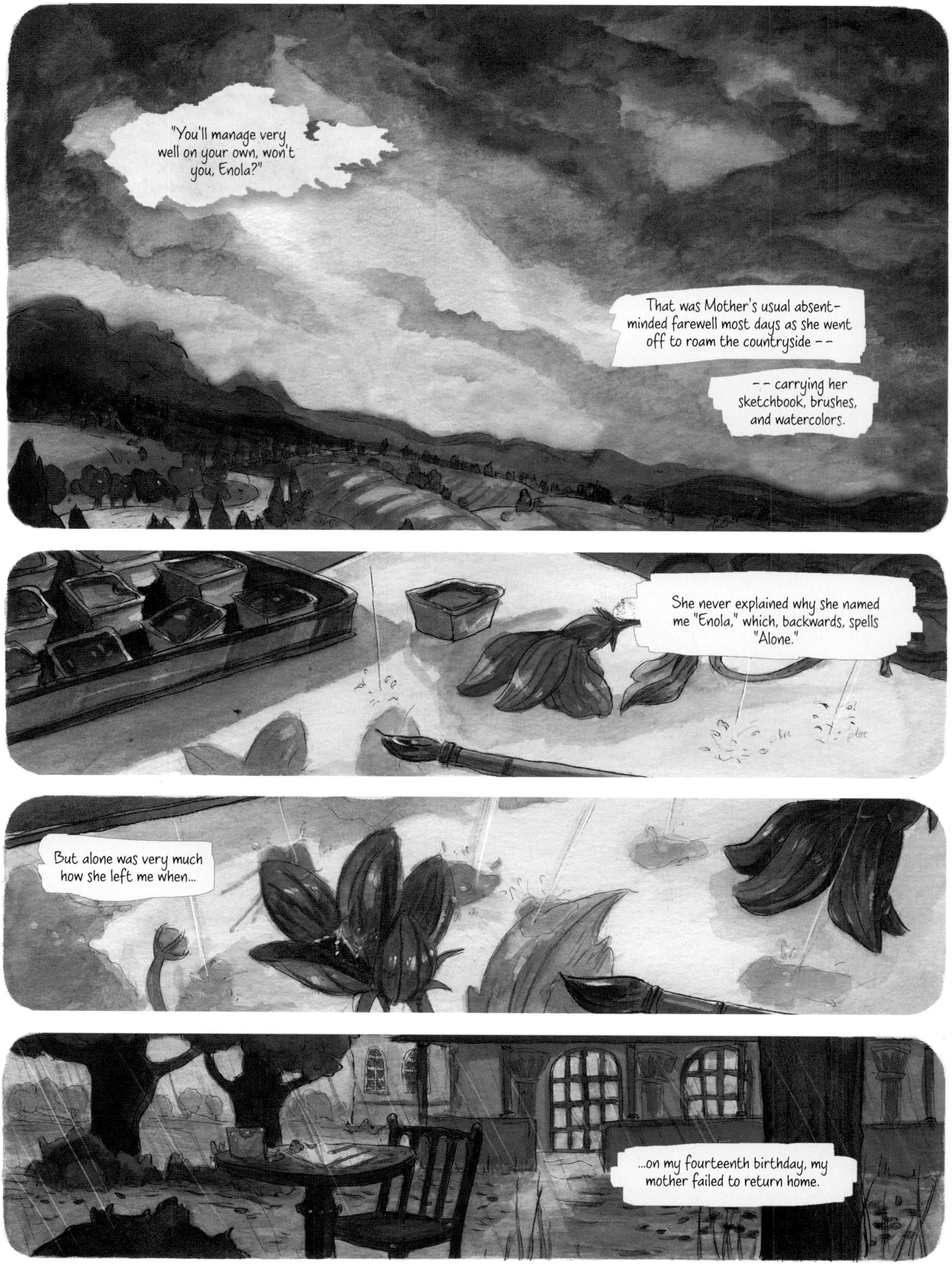
"You'll manage very well on your own, won't you, Enola?"
That was Mother's usual absent-minded farewell most days as she went off to roam the countryside --
-- carrying her sketchbook, brushes, and watercolors.
She never explained why she named me "Enola," which, backwards, spells "Alone."
But alone was very much how she left me when...
...on my fourteenth birthday, my mother failed to return home.

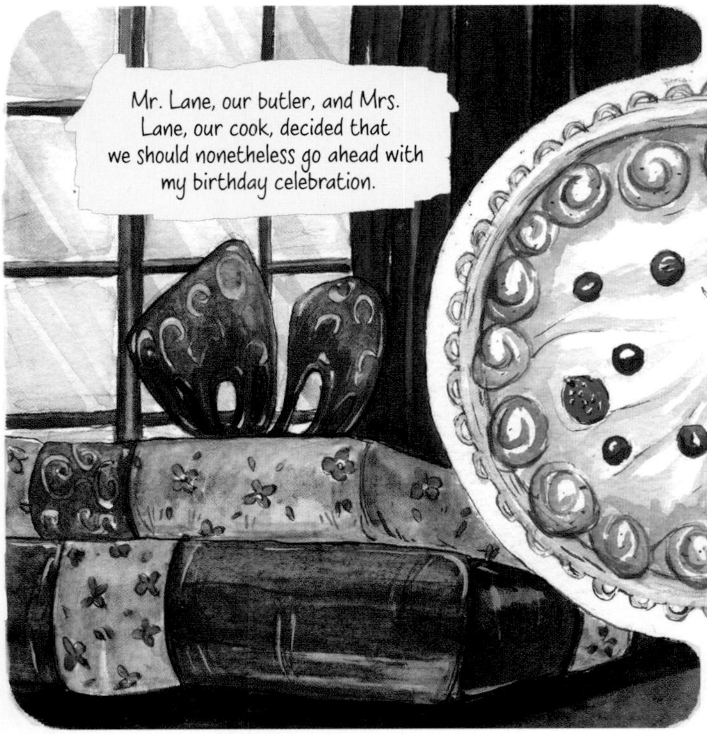
Mr. Lane, our butler, and Mrs. Lane, our cook, decided that we should nonetheless go ahead with my birthday celebration.

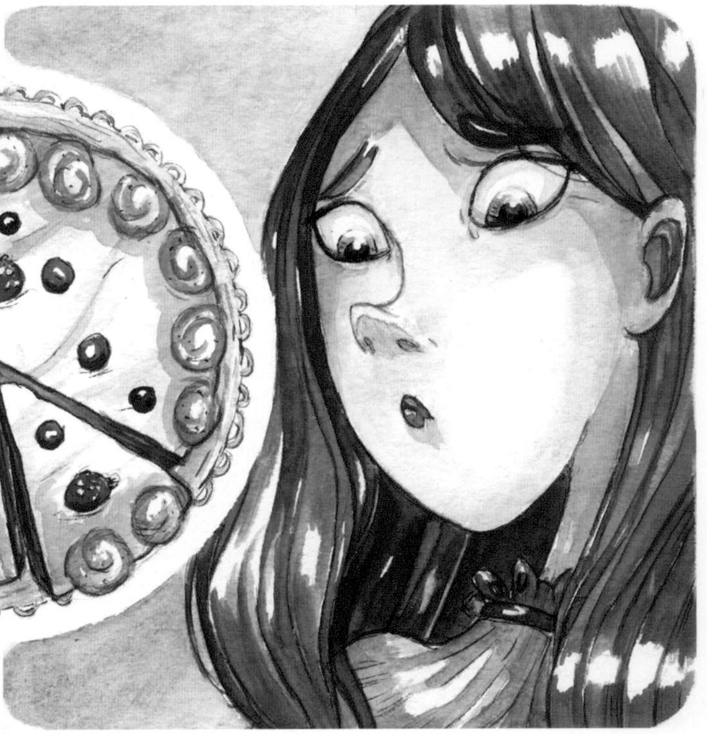

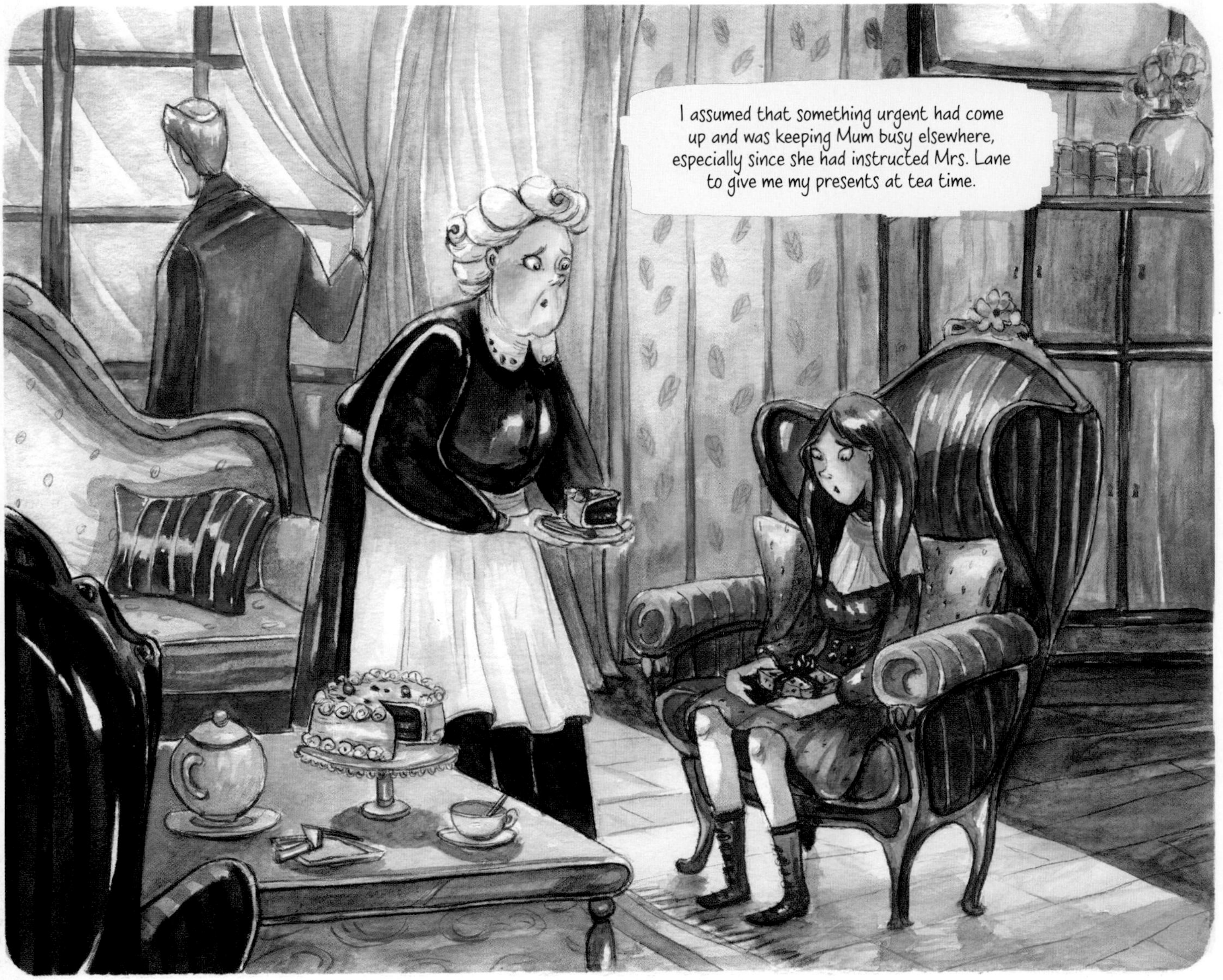
I assumed that something urgent had come up and was keeping Mum busy elsewhere, especially since she had instructed Mrs. Lane to give me my presents at tea time.

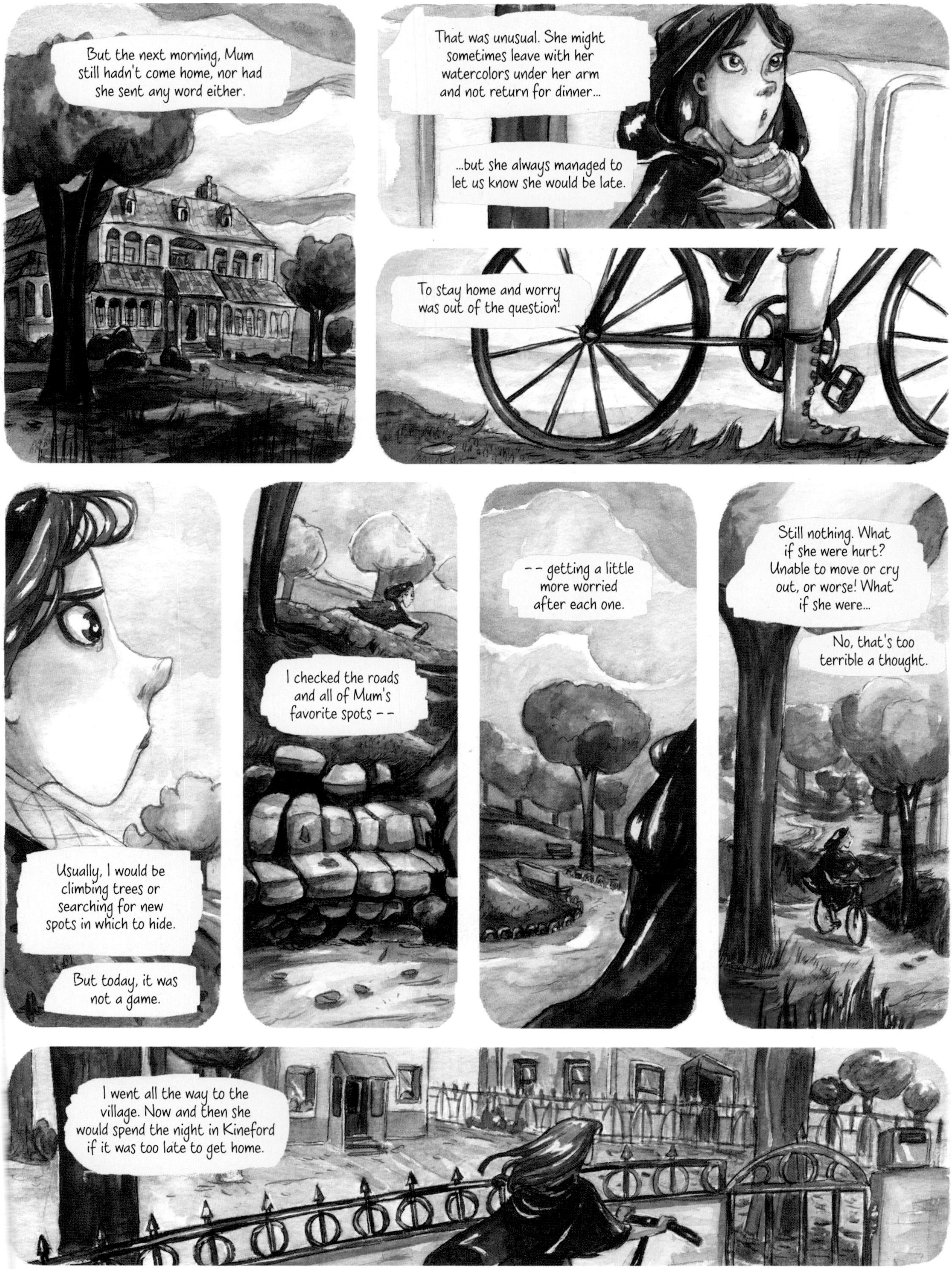
But the next morning, Mum still hadn't come home, nor had she sent any word either.
That was unusual. She might sometimes leave with her watercolors under her arm and not return for dinner...
...but she always managed to let us know she would be late.
To stay home and worry was out of the question!
Usually, I would be climbing trees or searching for new spots in which to hide.
But today, it was not a game.
I checked the roads and all of Mum's favorite spots --
-- getting a little more worried after each one.
Still nothing. What if she were hurt? Unable to move or cry out, or worse! What if she were...
No, that's too terrible a thought.
I went all the way to the village. Now and then she would spend the night in Kineford if it was too late to get home.

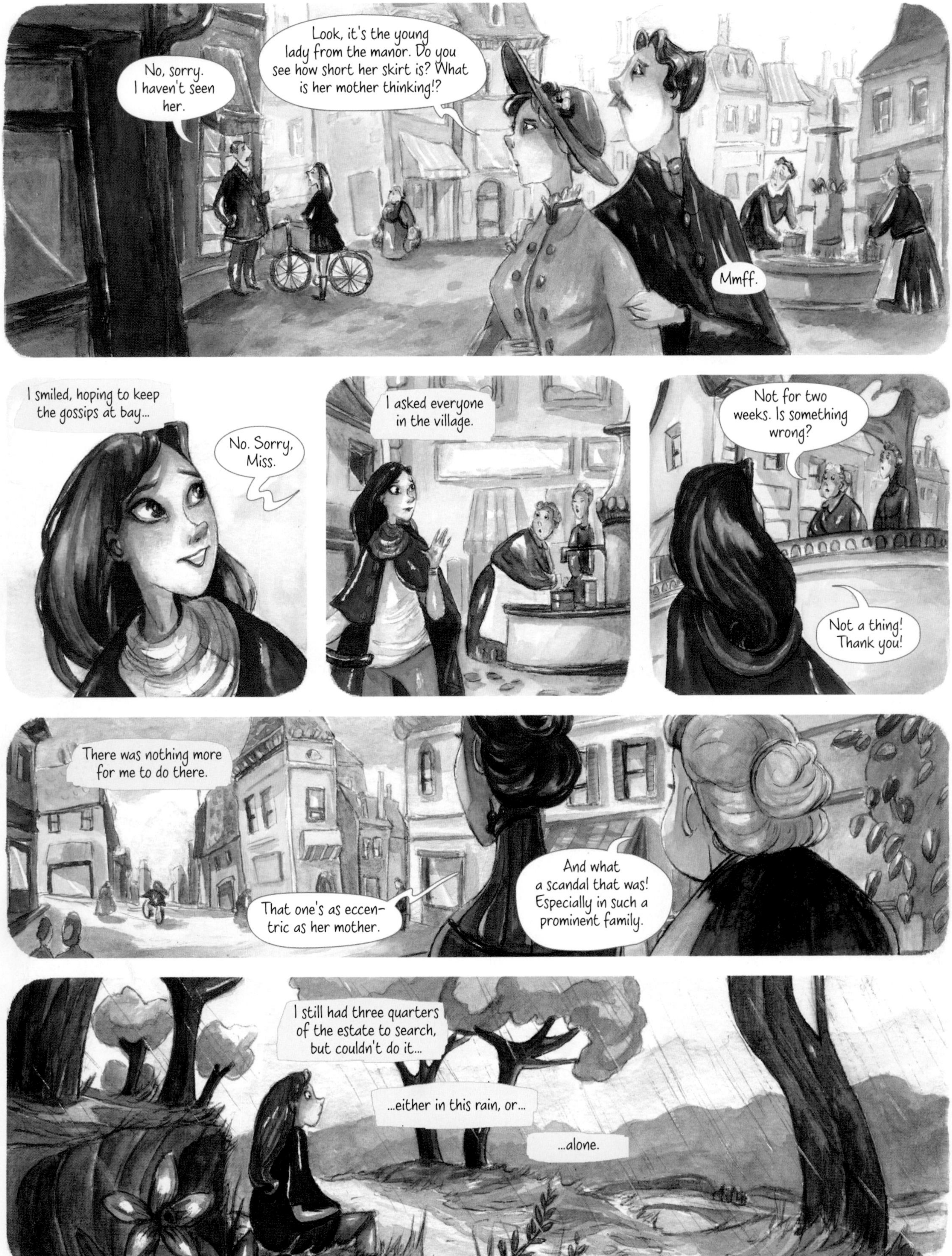
No, sorry. I haven't seen her.
Look, it's the young lady from the manor. Do you see how short her skirt is? What is her mother thinking!?
Mmff.
I smiled, hoping to keep the gossips at bay...
No. Sorry, Miss.
I asked everyone in the village.
Not for two weeks. Is something wrong?
Not a thing! Thank you!
There was nothing more for me to do there.
That one's as eccentric as her mother.
And what a scandal that was! Especially in such a prominent family.
I still had three quarters of the estate to search, but couldn't do it...
...either in this rain, or...
...alone.

Lady Holmes may be of an independent mind, but when there's a child, one doesn't spend the whole night out...

Mrs. Lane, I'm home.

Any news, Miss Enola?

No. Nobody has seen her. I couldn't find a trace of her anywhere.

You're soaked! Go sit by the stove!

And get brown like toast? No thanks!

Did Mr. Lane notify the police?

Yes, they're going to organize a search.

I have to send a telegram.

I'll light a fire for you in the library.

Did I really have to? Yes, I could put it off no longer.

Regardless that they haven't visited for ten years. A quarrel with Mum, I think...

...the shame of my late birth so many years after theirs. But the note must be sent...

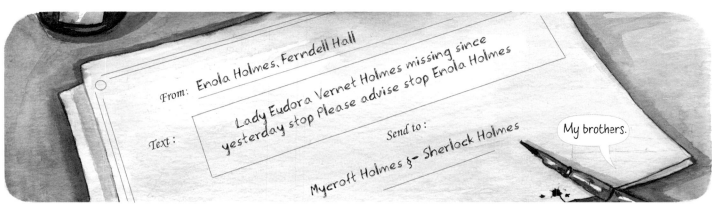

From: Enola Holmes, Ferndell Hall

Text: Lady Eudora Vernet Holmes missing since yesterday stop Please advise stop Enola Holmes

Send to: Mycroft Holmes & Sherlock Holmes

My brothers.

7

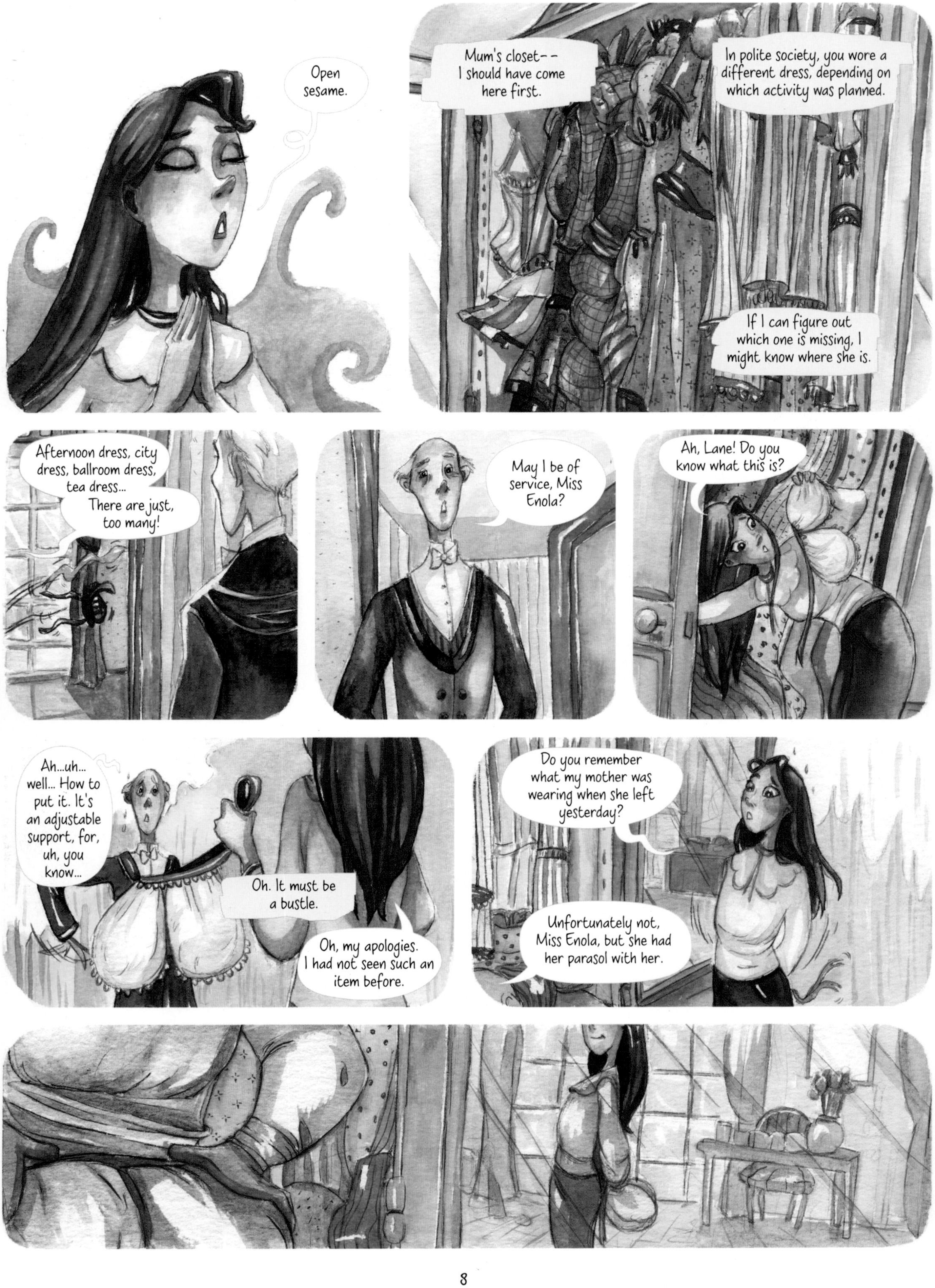
Open sesame.
Mum's closet-- I should have come here first.
In polite society, you wore a different dress, depending on which activity was planned.
If I can figure out which one is missing, I might know where she is.
Afternoon dress, city dress, ballroom dress, tea dress...
There are just, too many!
May I be of service, Miss Enola?
Ah, Lane! Do you know what this is?
Ah...uh... well... How to put it. It's an adjustable support, for, uh, you know...
Oh. It must be a bustle.
Oh, my apologies. I had not seen such an item before.
Do you remember what my mother was wearing when she left yesterday?
Unfortunately not, Miss Enola, but she had her parasol with her.

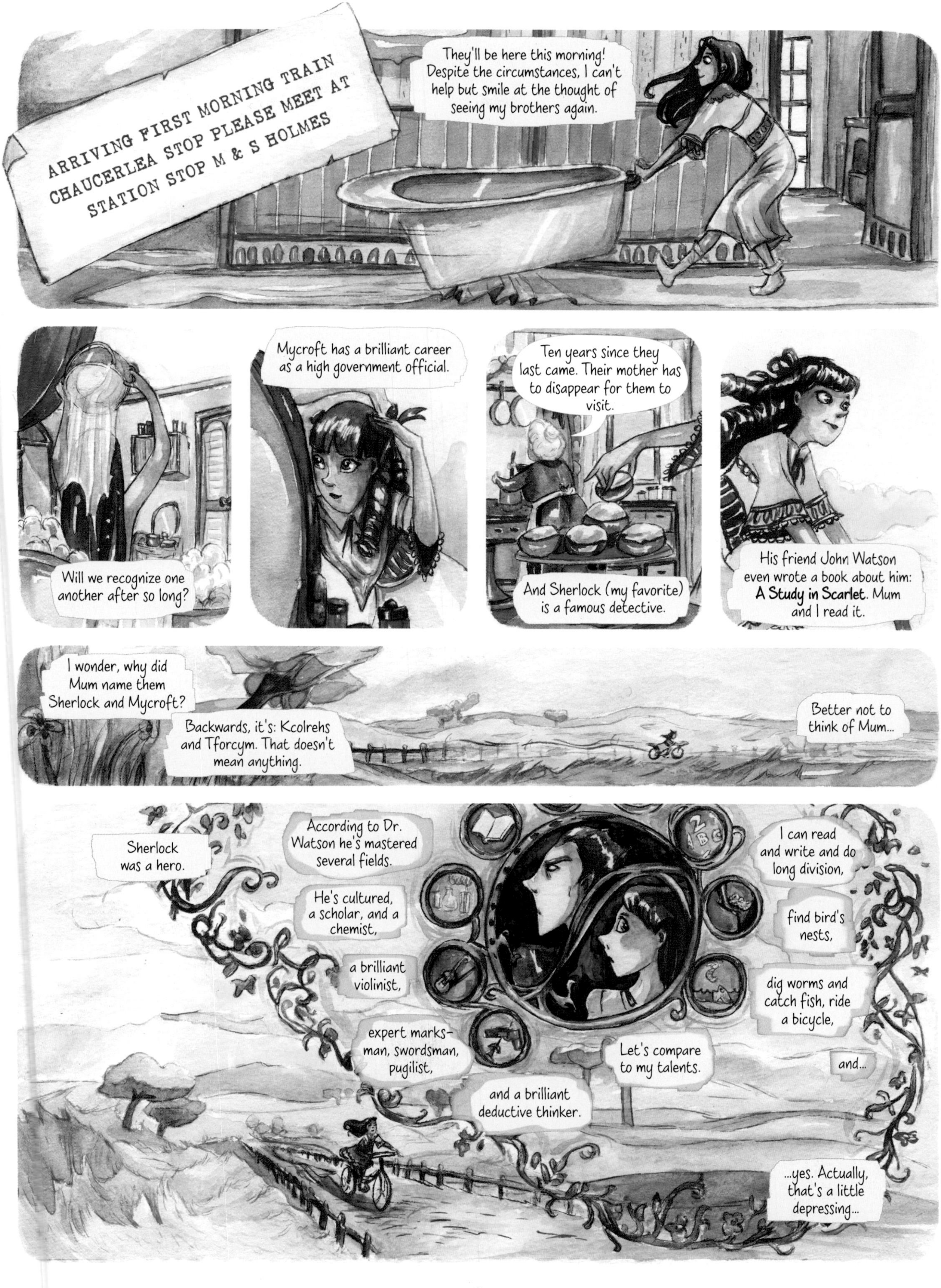

ARRIVING FIRST MORNING TRAIN CHAUCERLEA STOP PLEASE MEET AT STATION STOP M & S HOLMES
They'll be here this morning! Despite the circumstances, I can't help but smile at the thought of seeing my brothers again.
Will we recognize one another after so long?
Mycroft has a brilliant career as a high government official.
Ten years since they last came. Their mother has to disappear for them to visit.
And Sherlock (my favorite) is a famous detective.
His friend John Watson even wrote a book about him: **A Study in Scarlet**. Mum and I read it.
I wonder, why did Mum name them Sherlock and Mycroft?
Backwards, it's: Kcolrehs and Tforcym. That doesn't mean anything.
Better not to think of Mum...
Sherlock was a hero.
According to Dr. Watson he's mastered several fields.
He's cultured, a scholar, and a chemist,
a brilliant violinist,
expert marks-man, swordsman, pugilist,
and a brilliant deductive thinker.
Let's compare to my talents.
I can read and write and do long division,
find bird's nests,
dig worms and catch fish, ride a bicycle,
and...
...yes. Actually, that's a little depressing...

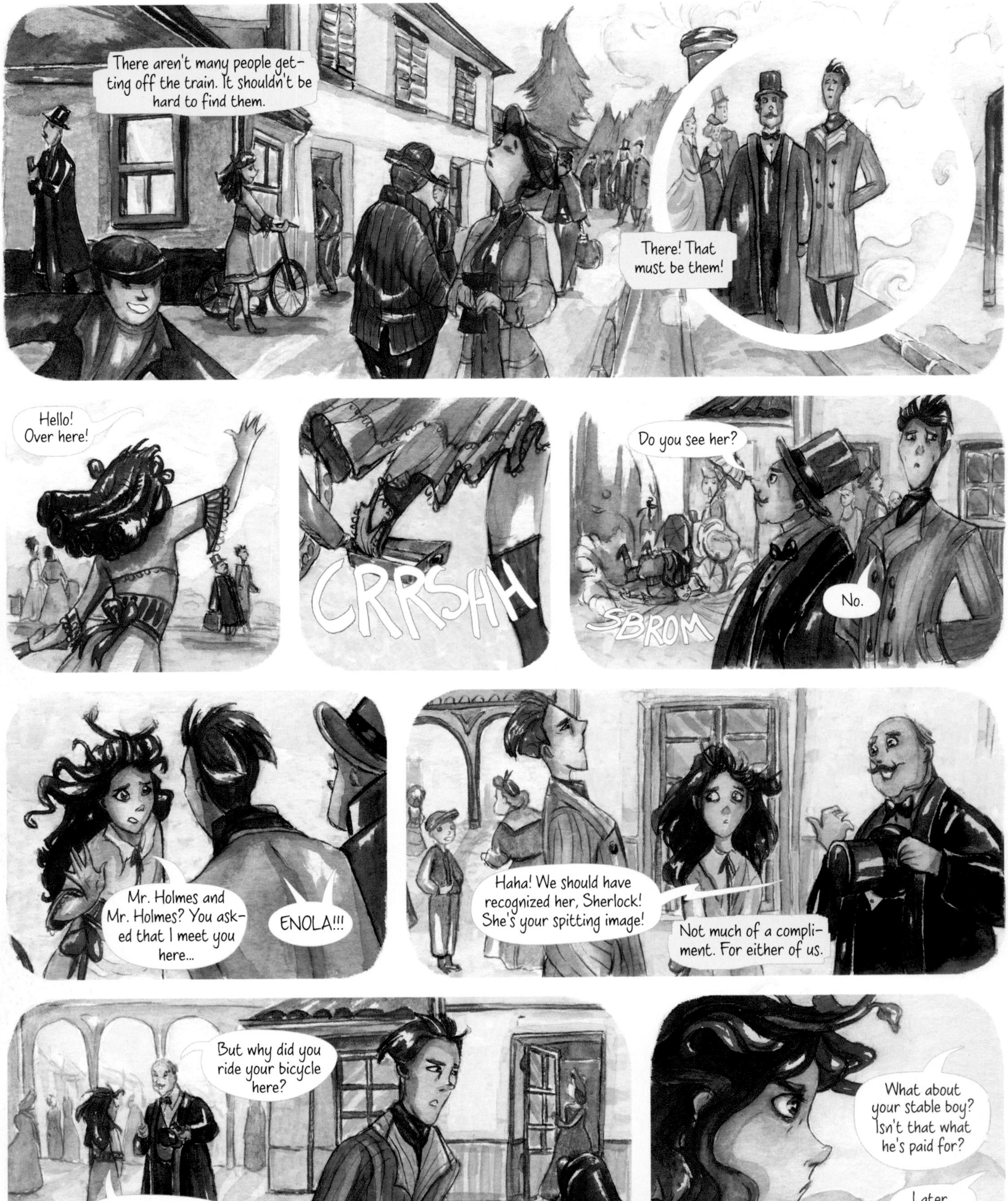

There aren't many people getting off the train. It shouldn't be hard to find them.
There! That must be them!
Hello! Over here!
CRRSAH
Do you see her?
SBROM
No.
Mr. Holmes and Mr. Holmes? You asked that I meet you here...
ENOLA!!!
Haha! We should have recognized her, Sherlock! She's your spitting image!
Not much of a compliment. For either of us.
But why did you ride your bicycle here?
I guess I could have rented horses, but I wouldn't have known how to hitch them.
Go get us a cab, young man.
What about your stable boy? Isn't that what he's paid for?
Later, Mycroft.
Why don't we go wait inside the station. The wind is making a crow's nest of Enola's hair.

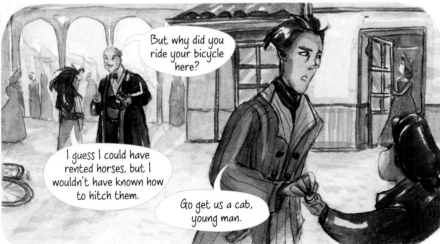

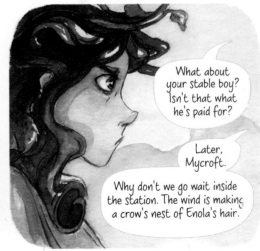

And what about your gloves, Enola? Is that really how a young lady should dress?

I'm only fourteen!

You should have been in a dress since you were twelve.

Besides, I'm paying the seamstress a fortune for you and Mother.

A "Hello, good to see you again, Enola" would have been nice...

What is our mother up to? I bet she's joined up with the suffragettes*.

Mother...

?!?

We are a pair of thoughtless brutes. It's clearly painful for you to think about our mother.

Do you think you are feeling well enough to tell us the facts so far?

Yes, Mum left Tuesday morning, without leaving a message, and hasn't come home since.

Was she unwell?

No.

Have you discovered any blood or signs of a break-in?

None.

Any suspicious figures, or possible enemies?

Not that I know of, but we alerted the Kineford police.

And they're already here, clumsily going about their investigation. As usual...

Ha! What are they expecting? That she's been hiding in a bush?

* Suffragettes were women activists who led the fight for women's right to vote.

11

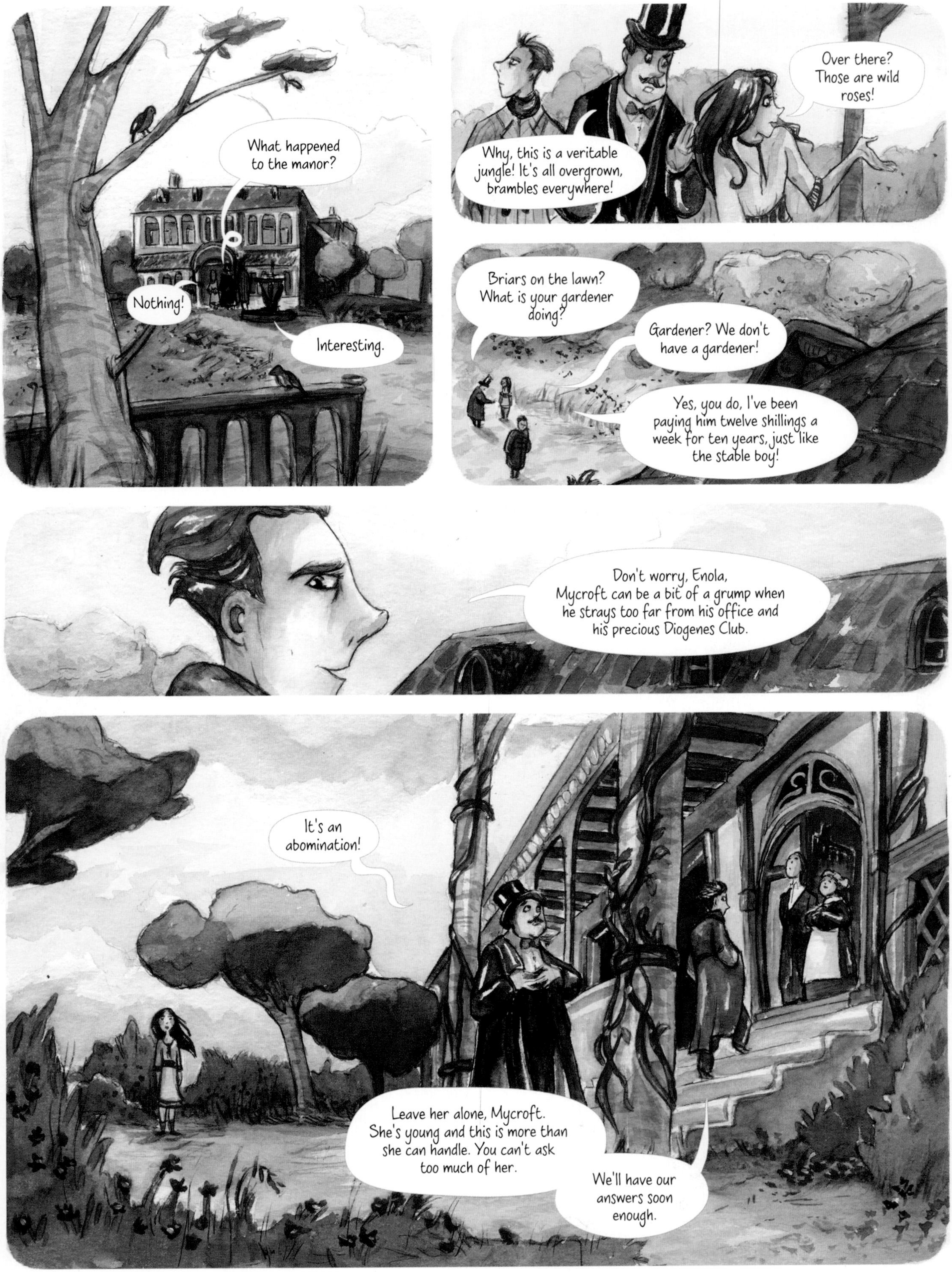
What happened to the manor?
Nothing!
Interesting.
Why, this is a veritable jungle! It's all overgrown, brambles everywhere!
Over there? Those are wild roses!
Briars on the lawn? What is your gardener doing?
Gardener? We don't have a gardener!
Yes, you do, I've been paying him twelve shillings a week for ten years, just like the stable boy!
Don't worry, Enola, Mycroft can be a bit of a grump when he strays too far from his office and his precious Diogenes Club.
It's an abomination!
Leave her alone, Mycroft. She's young and this is more than she can handle. You can't ask too much of her.
We'll have our answers soon enough.

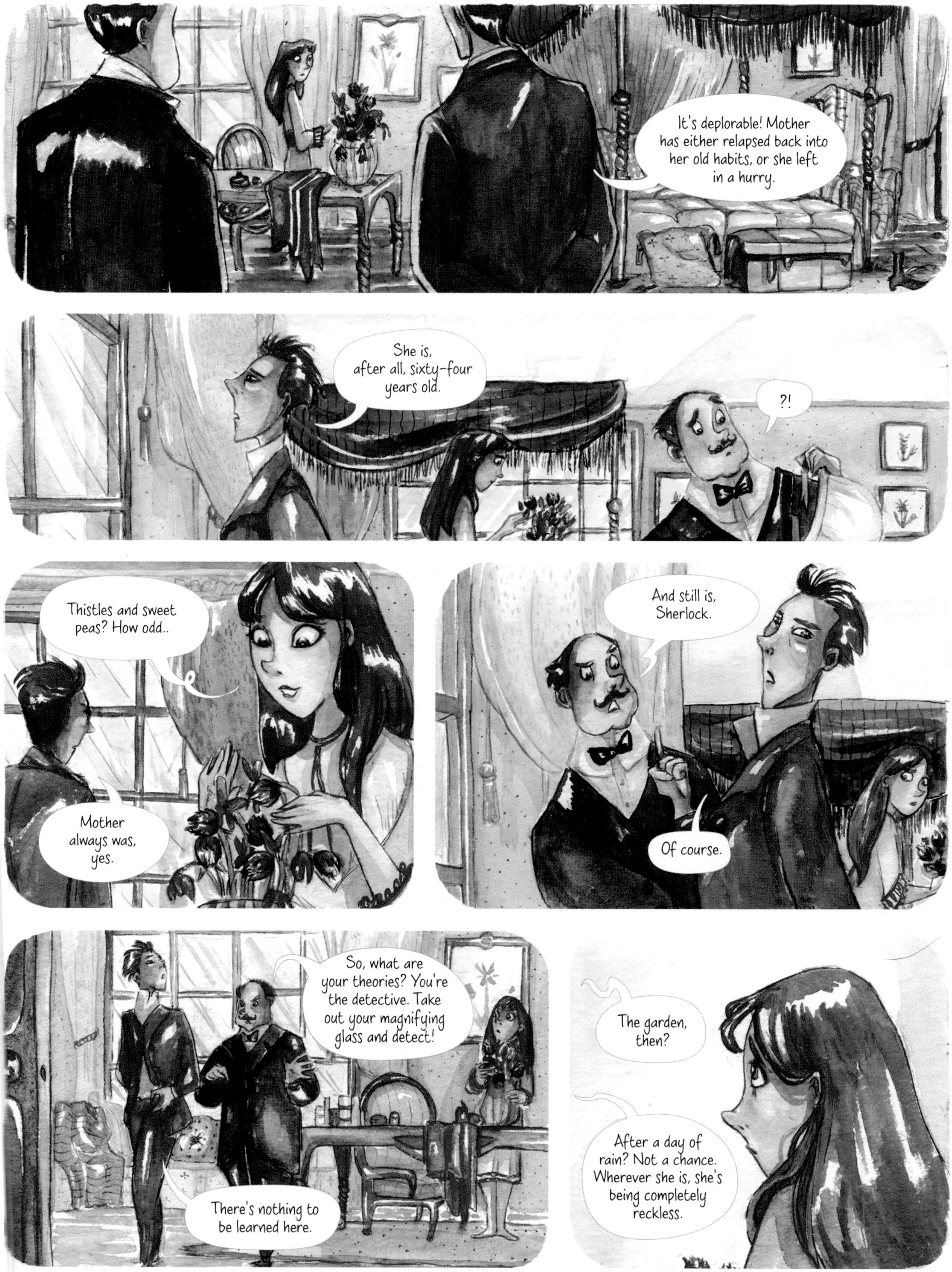
It's deplorable! Mother has either relapsed back into her old habits, or she left in a hurry.
She is, after all, sixty-four years old.
?!
Thistles and sweet peas? How odd..
Mother always was, yes.
And still is, Sherlock.
Of course.
So, what are your theories? You're the detective. Take out your magnifying glass and detect!
There's nothing to be learned here.
The garden, then?
After a day of rain? Not a chance. Wherever she is, she's being completely reckless.

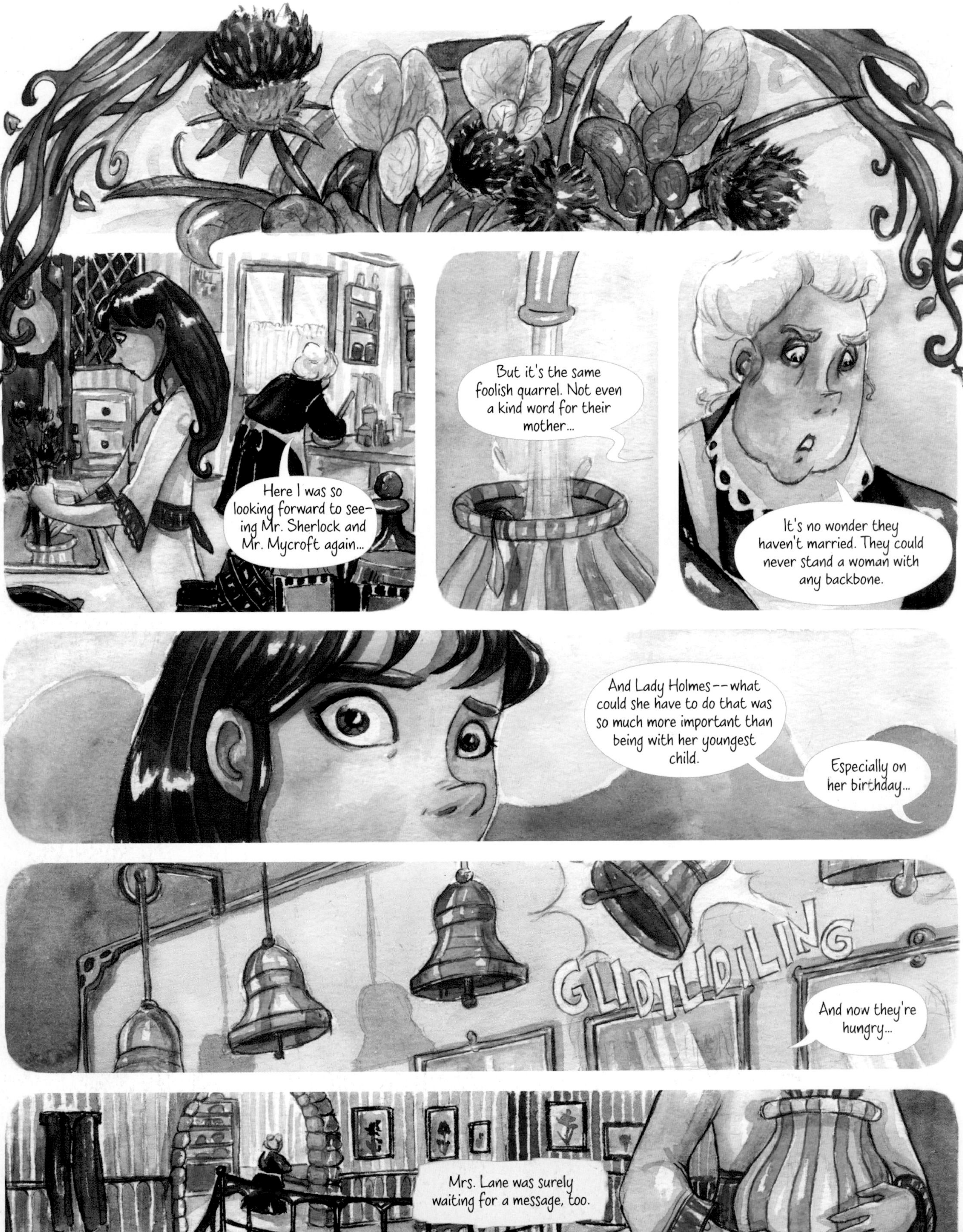
Here I was so looking forward to seeing Mr. Sherlock and Mr. Mycroft again...
But it's the same foolish quarrel. Not even a kind word for their mother...
It's no wonder they haven't married. They could never stand a woman with any backbone.
And Lady Holmes--what could she have to do that was so much more important than being with her youngest child.
Especially on her birthday...
GLIDILIDILING
And now they're hungry...
Mrs. Lane was surely waiting for a message, too.

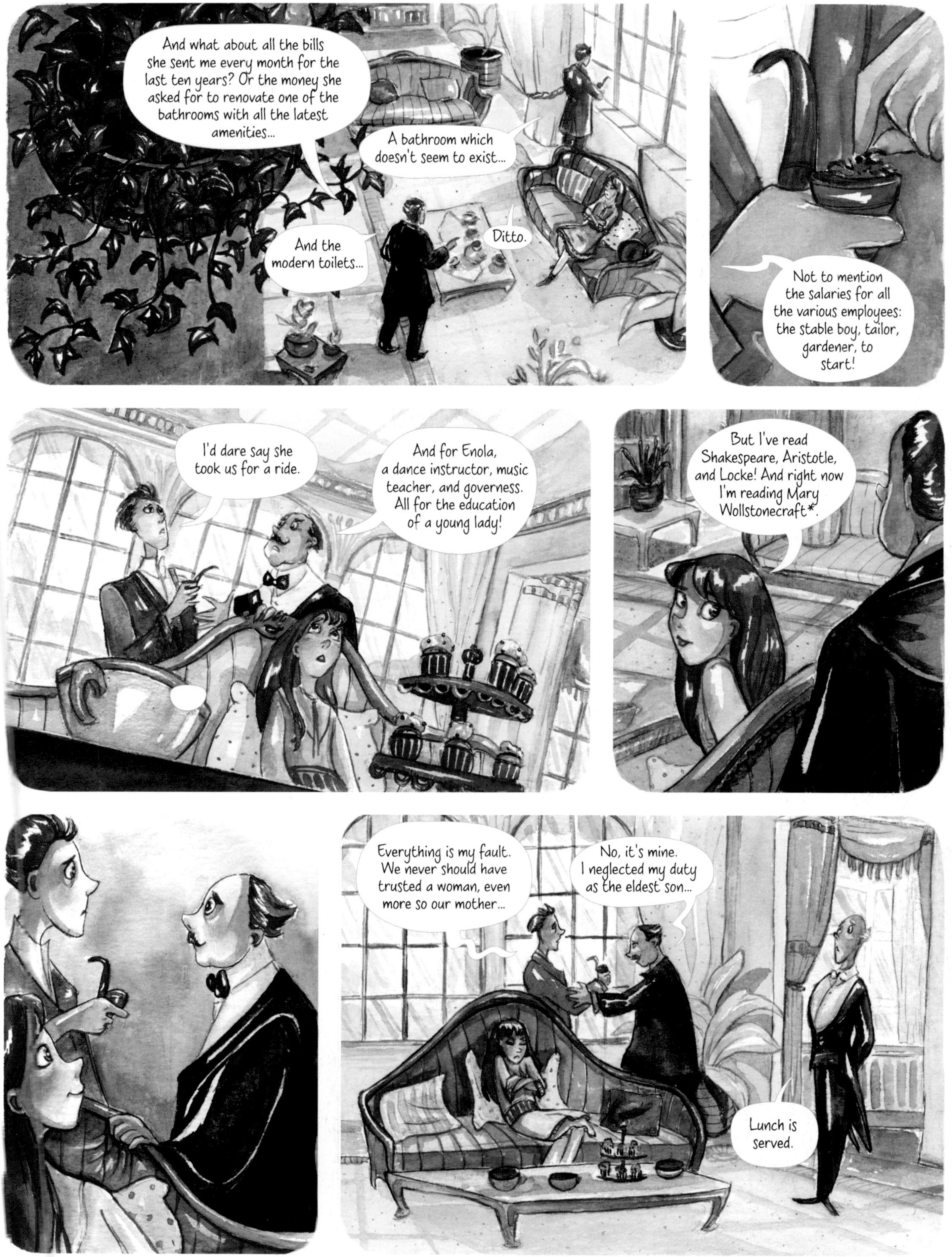

And what about all the bills she sent me every month for the last ten years? Or the money she asked for to renovate one of the bathrooms with all the latest amenities...
A bathroom which doesn't seem to exist...
Ditto.
And the modern toilets...
Not to mention the salaries for all the various employees: the stable boy, tailor, gardener, to start!
I'd dare say she took us for a ride.
And for Enola, a dance instructor, music teacher, and governess. All for the education of a young lady!
But I've read Shakespeare, Aristotle, and Locke! And right now I'm reading Mary Wollstonecraft*.
Everything is my fault. We never should have trusted a woman, even more so our mother...
No, it's mine. I neglected my duty as the eldest son...
Lunch is served.

* A British writer and one of the pioneers of the feminist movement.

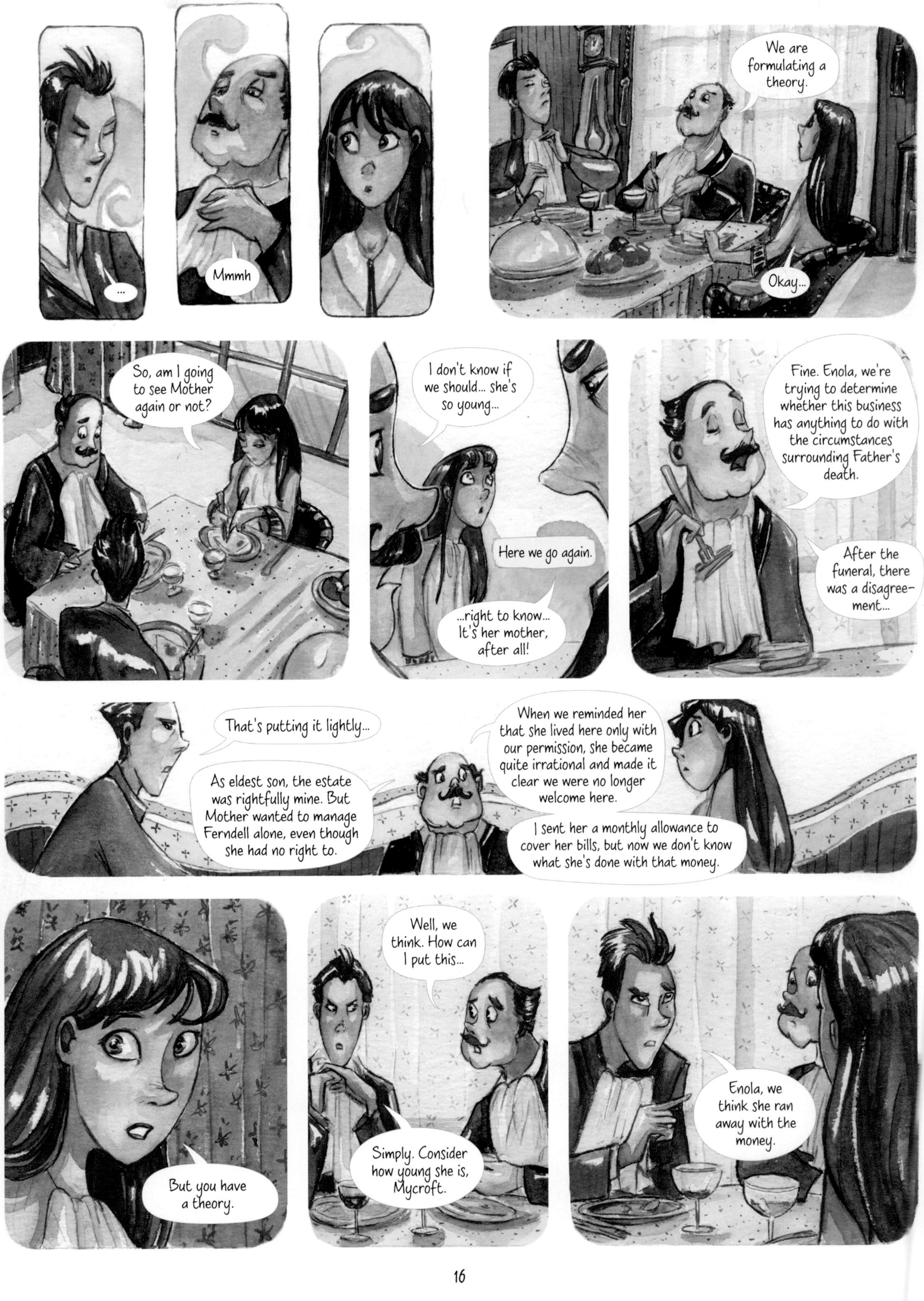
...
Mmmh
We are formulating a theory.
Okay...
So, am I going to see Mother again or not?
I don't know if we should... she's so young...
Here we go again.
...right to know... It's her mother, after all!
Fine. Enola, we're trying to determine whether this business has anything to do with the circumstances surrounding Father's death.
After the funeral, there was a disagreement...
That's putting it lightly...
As eldest son, the estate was rightfully mine. But Mother wanted to manage Ferndell alone, even though she had no right to.
When we reminded her that she lived here only with our permission, she became quite irrational and made it clear we were no longer welcome here.
I sent her a monthly allowance to cover her bills, but now we don't know what she's done with that money.
But you have a theory.
Well, we think. How can I put this...
Simply. Consider how young she is, Mycroft.
Enola, we think she ran away with the money.

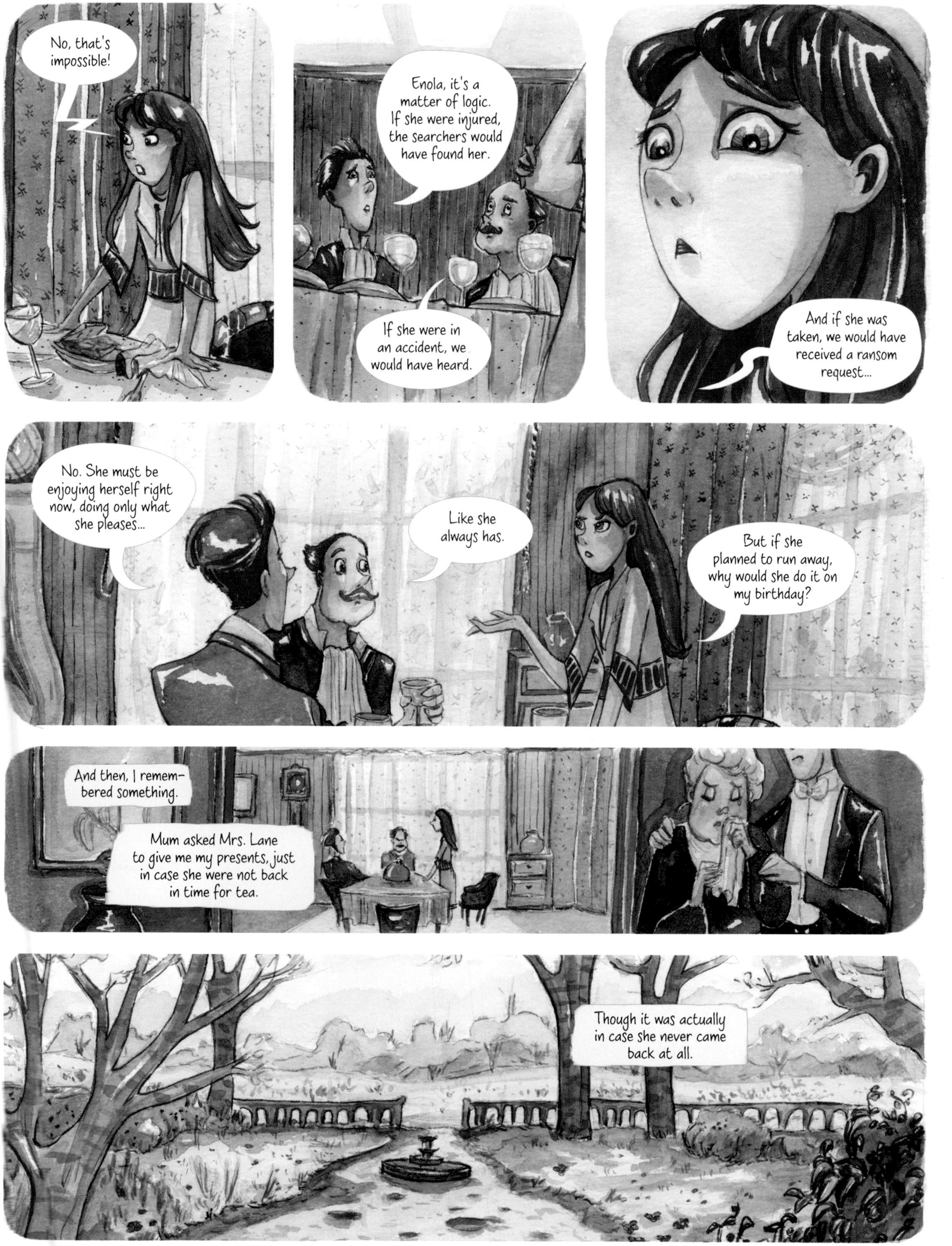
No, that's impossible!
Enola, it's a matter of logic. If she were injured, the searchers would have found her.
If she were in an accident, we would have heard.
And if she was taken, we would have received a ransom request...
No. She must be enjoying herself right now, doing only what she pleases...
Like she always has.
But if she planned to run away, why would she do it on my birthday?
And then, I remembered something.
Mum asked Mrs. Lane to give me my presents, just in case she were not back in time for tea.
Though it was actually in case she never came back at all.

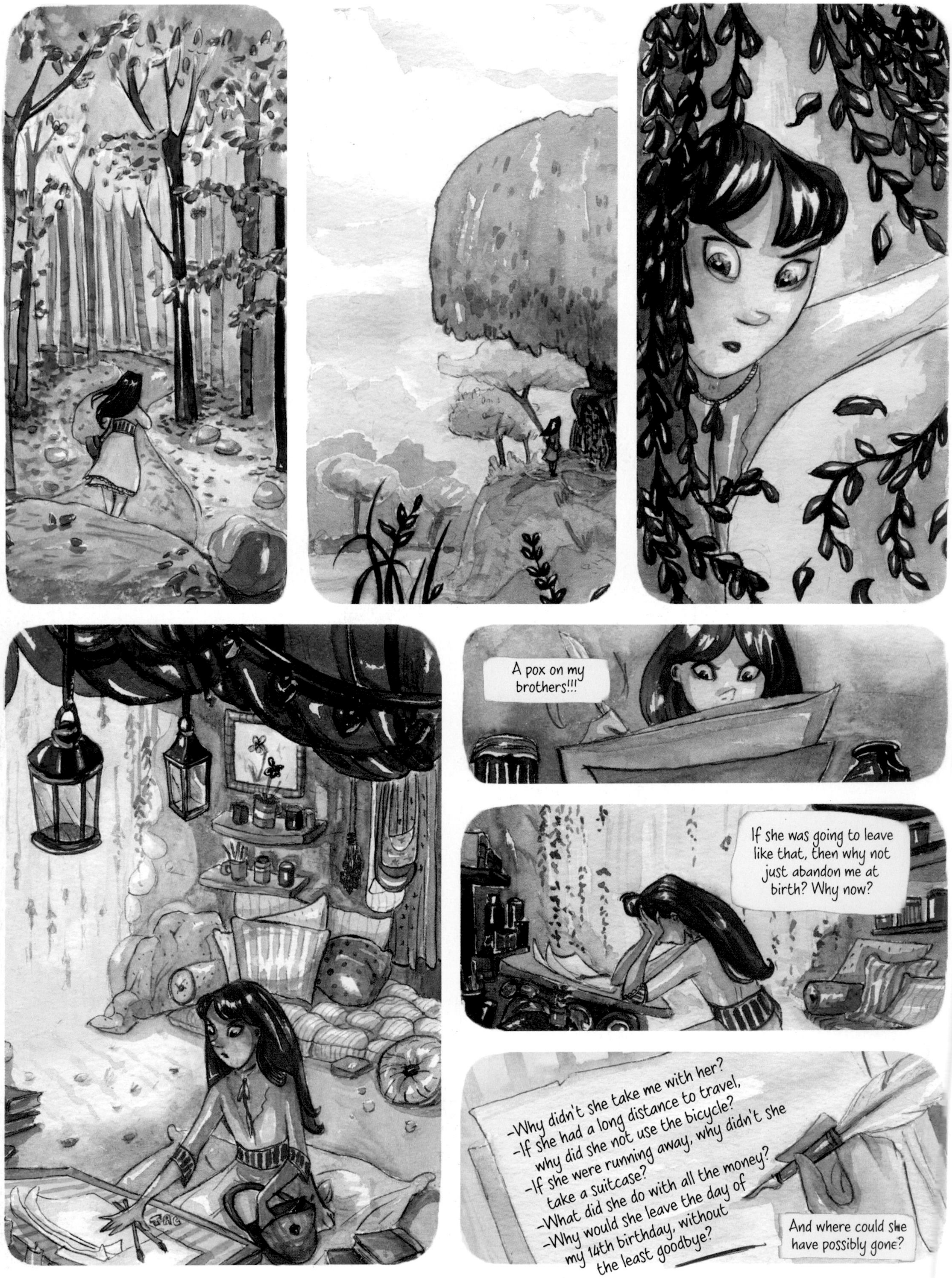
A pox on my brothers!!!
If she was going to leave like that, then why not just abandon me at birth? Why now?
-Why didn't she take me with her?
-If she had a long distance to travel, why did she not use the bicycle?
-If she were running away, why didn't she take a suitcase?
-What did she do with all the money?
-Why would she leave the day of my 14th birthday, without the least goodbye?
And where could she have possibly gone?

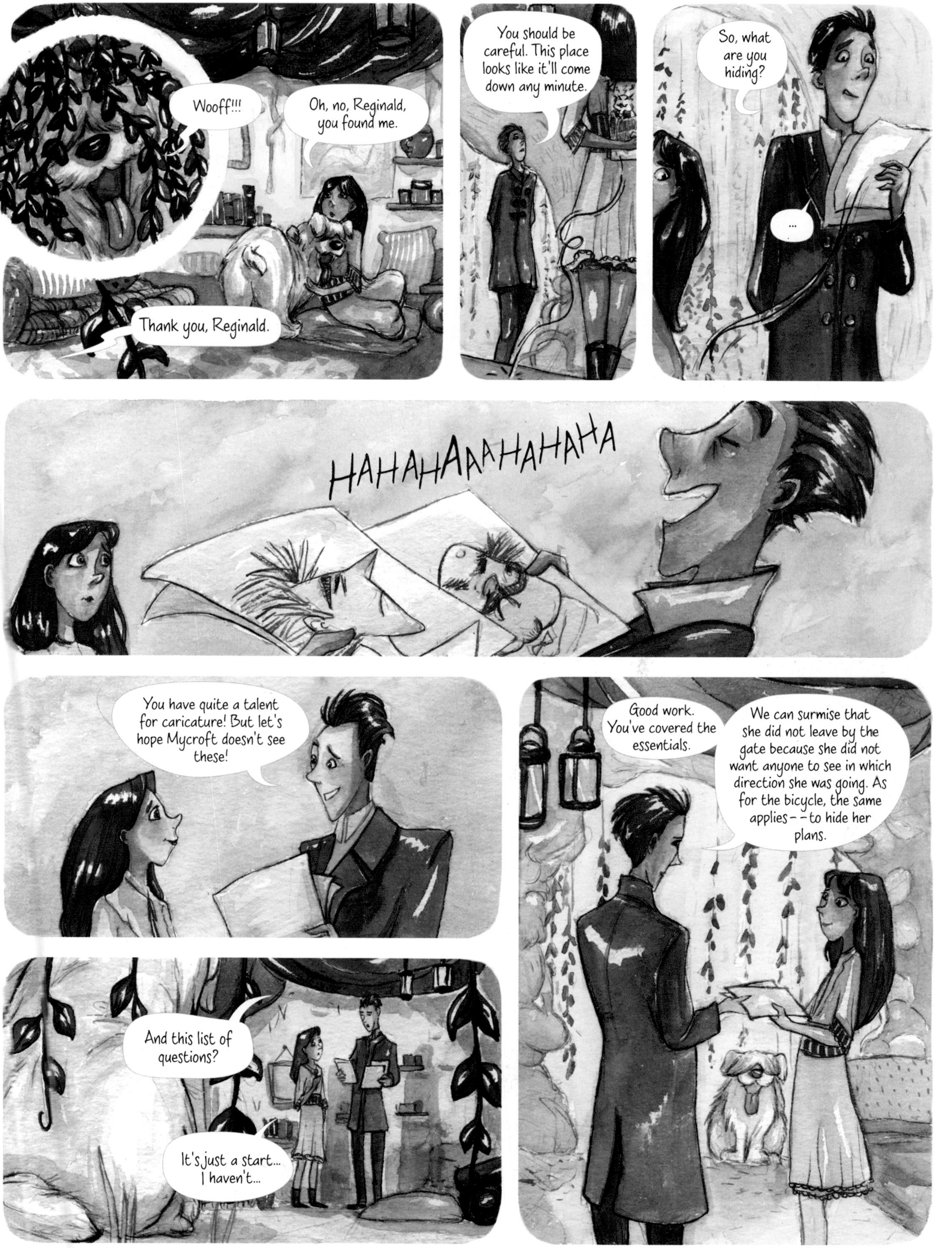
Wooff!!!
Oh, no, Reginald, you found me.
Thank you, Reginald.
You should be careful. This place looks like it'll come down any minute.
So, what are you hiding?
...
HAHAHAAAAHAHAHA
You have quite a talent for caricature! But let's hope Mycroft doesn't see these!
And this list of questions?
It's just a start... I haven't...
Good work. You've covered the essentials.
We can surmise that she did not leave by the gate because she did not want anyone to see in which direction she was going. As for the bicycle, the same applies--to hide her plans.

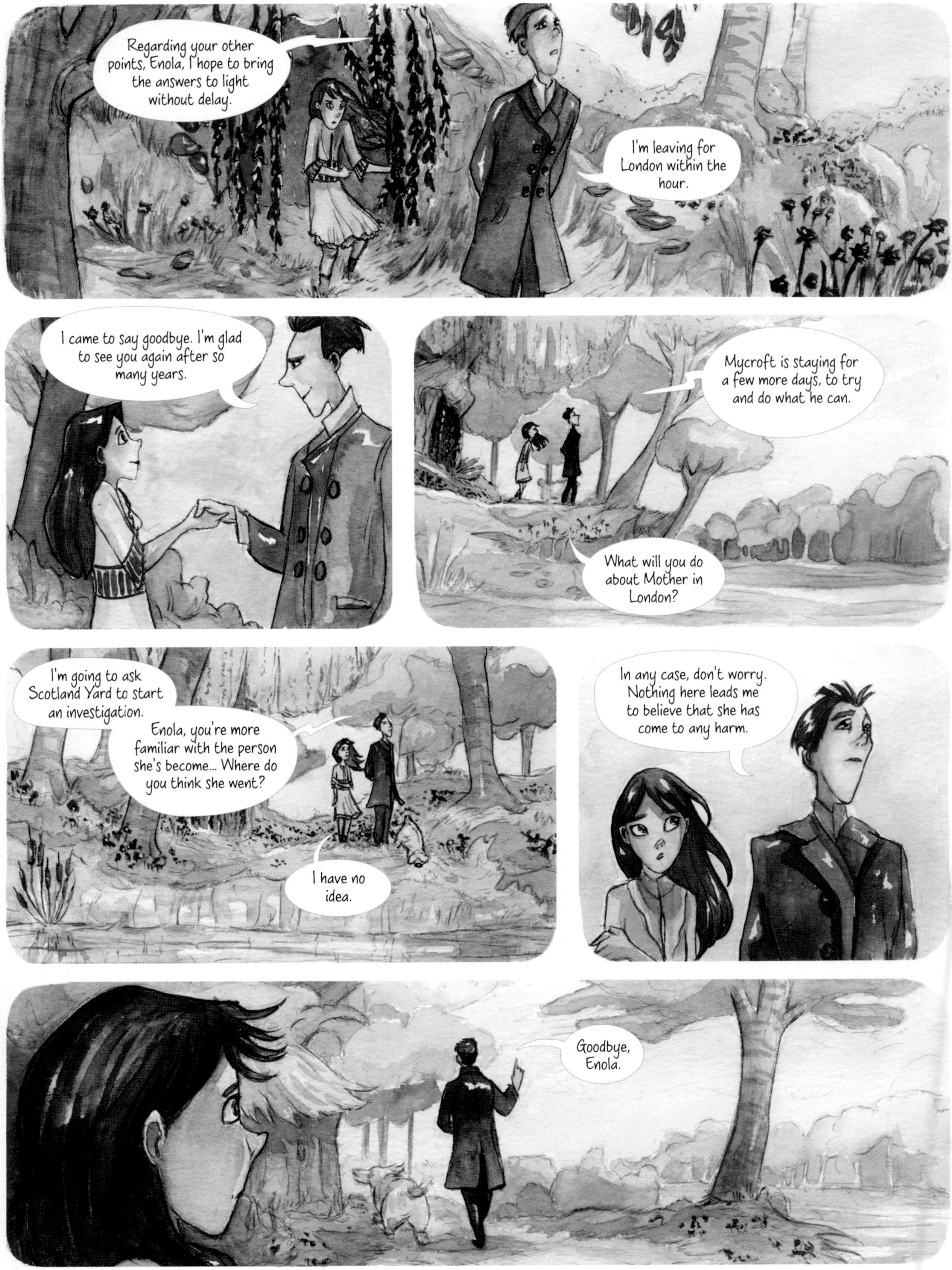
Regarding your other points, Enola, I hope to bring the answers to light without delay.
I'm leaving for London within the hour.
I came to say goodbye. I'm glad to see you again after so many years.
Mycroft is staying for a few more days, to try and do what he can.
What will you do about Mother in London?
I'm going to ask Scotland Yard to start an investigation.
Enola, you're more familiar with the person she's become... Where do you think she went?
I have no idea.
In any case, don't worry. Nothing here leads me to believe that she has come to any harm.
Goodbye, Enola.

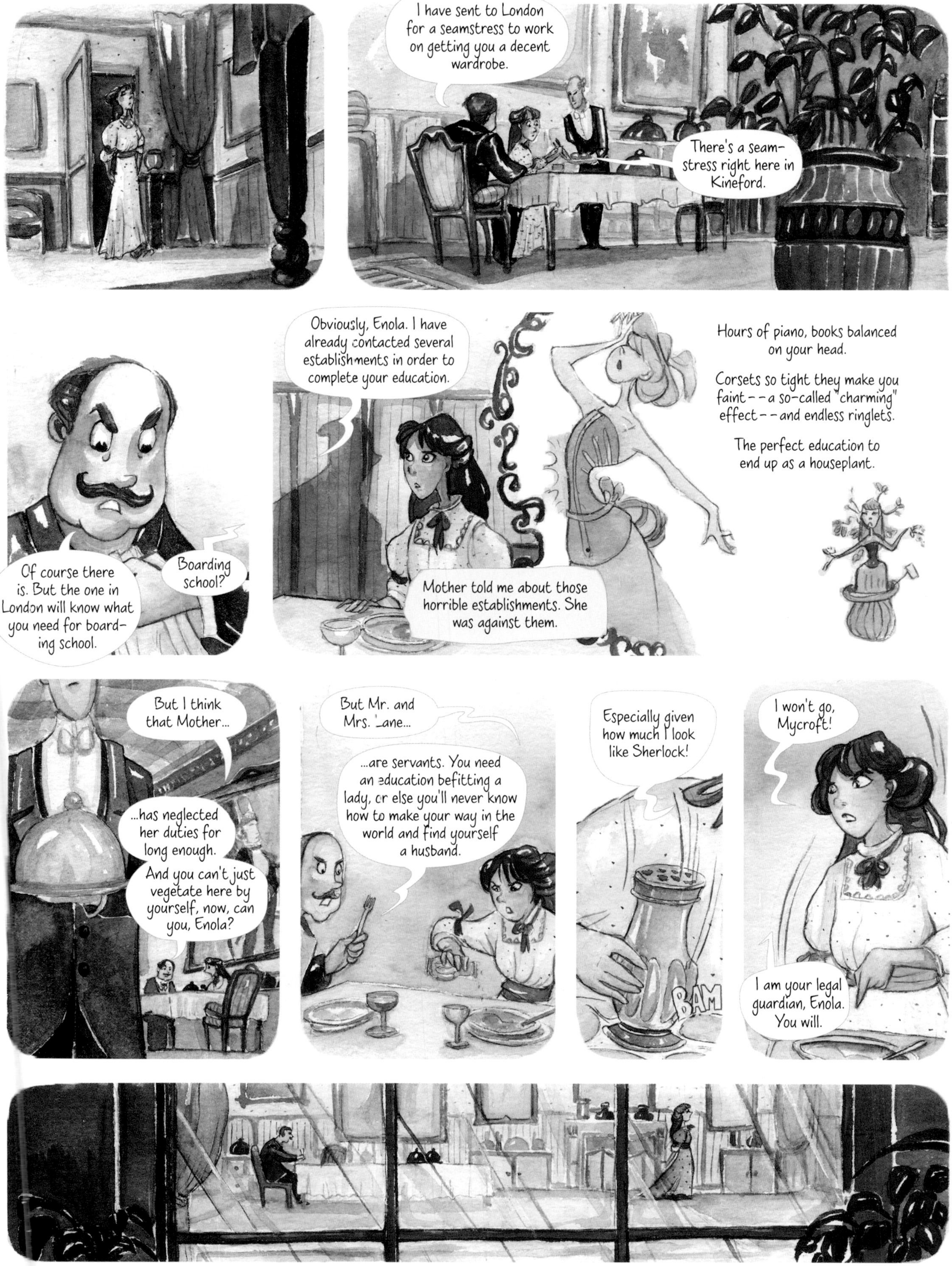
I have sent to London for a seamstress to work on getting you a decent wardrobe.
There's a seamstress right here in Kineford.
Of course there is. But the one in London will know what you need for boarding school.
Boarding school?
Obviously, Enola. I have already contacted several establishments in order to complete your education.
Mother told me about those horrible establishments. She was against them.
Hours of piano, books balanced on your head.
Corsets so tight they make you faint--a so-called "charming" effect--and endless ringlets.
The perfect education to end up as a houseplant.
But I think that Mother...
...has neglected her duties for long enough.
And you can't just vegetate here by yourself, now, can you, Enola?
But Mr. and Mrs. Lane...
...are servants. You need an education befitting a lady, or else you'll never know how to make your way in the world and find yourself a husband.
Especially given how much I look like Sherlock!
BAM
I won't go, Mycroft!
I am your legal guardian, Enola. You will.

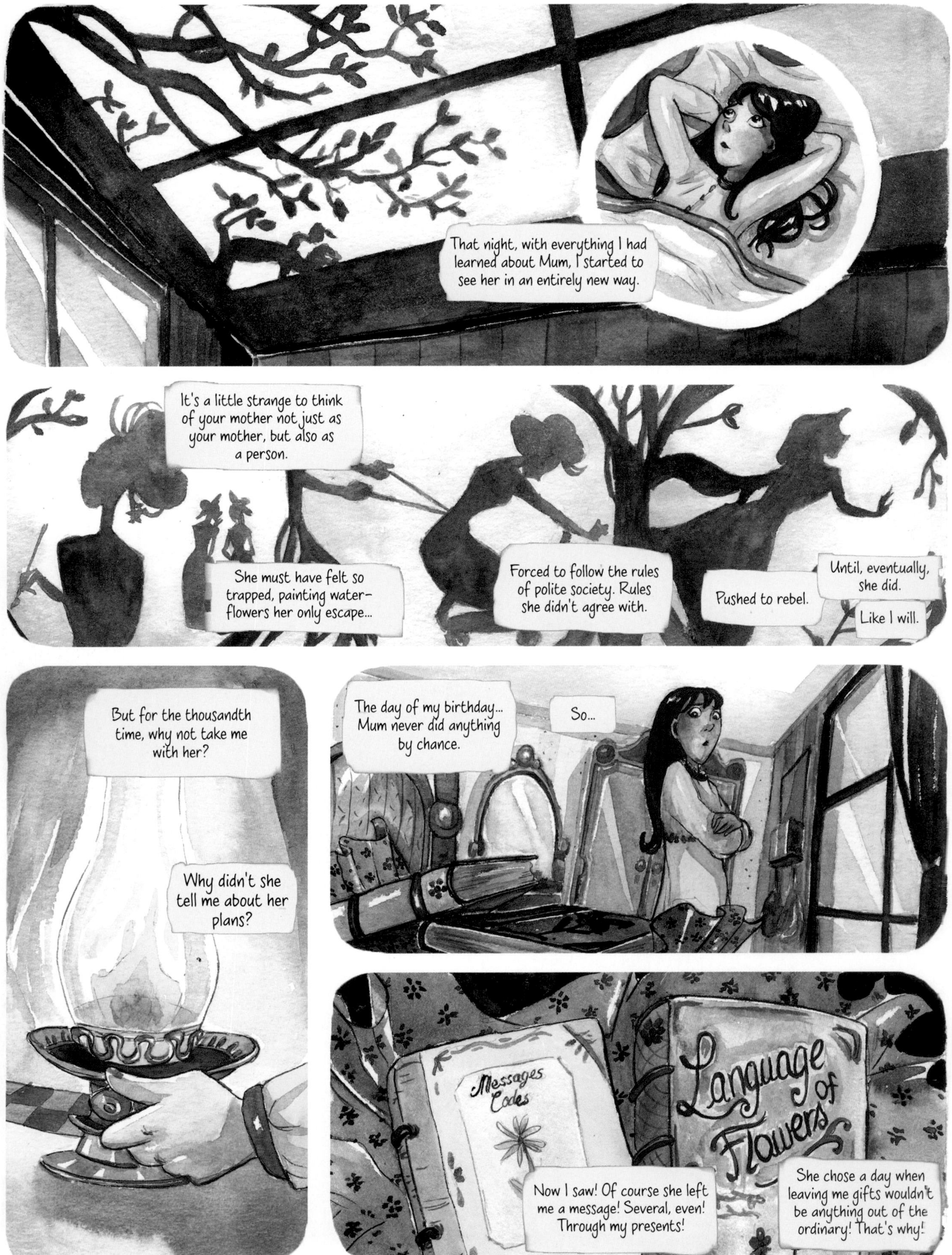
That night, with everything I had learned about Mum, I started to see her in an entirely new way.
It's a little strange to think of your mother not just as your mother, but also as a person.
She must have felt so trapped, painting water-flowers her only escape...
Forced to follow the rules of polite society. Rules she didn't agree with.
Pushed to rebel.
Until, eventually, she did.
Like I will.
But for the thousandth time, why not take me with her?
Why didn't she tell me about her plans?
The day of my birthday... Mum never did anything by chance.
So...
Messages
Codes
Language of Flowers
Now I saw! Of course she left me a message! Several, even! Through my presents!
She chose a day when leaving me gifts wouldn't be anything out of the ordinary! That's why!

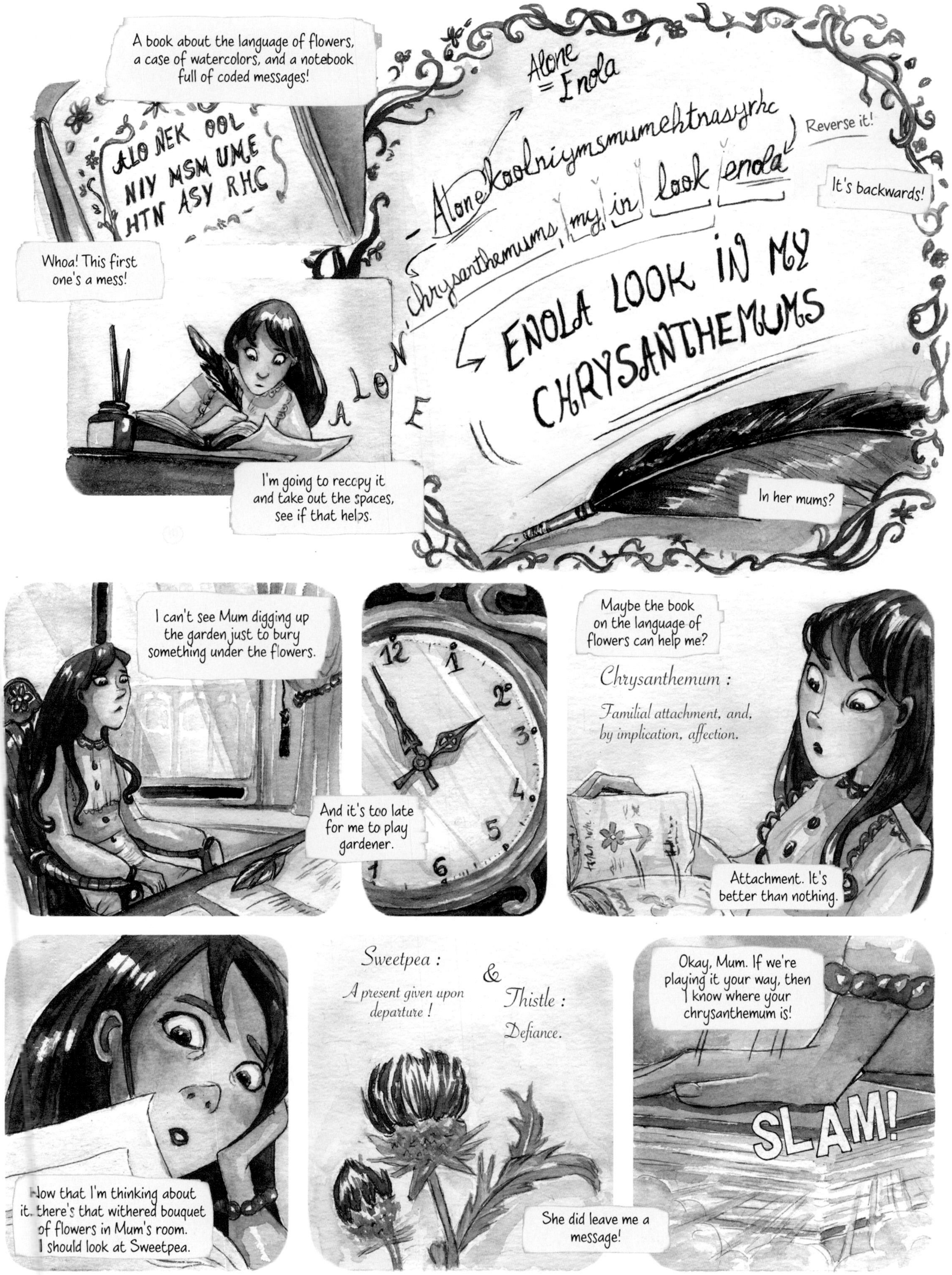

A book about the language of flowers, a case of watercolors, and a notebook full of coded messages!
ALO NEK OOL
NIY MSM UME
HTN ASY RHC
Whoa! This first one's a mess!
A L O N E
I'm going to recopy it and take out the spaces, see if that helps.
Alone
= Enola
Alonekoolniymsmumehtnasyrhc
Reverse it!
chrysanthemums my in look enola
It's backwards!
ENOLA LOOK IN MY CHRYSANTHEMUMS
In her mums?
I can't see Mum digging up the garden just to bury something under the flowers.
And it's too late for me to play gardener.
Maybe the book on the language of flowers can help me?
Chrysanthemum :
Familial attachment, and, by implication, affection.
Attachment. It's better than nothing.
Now that I'm thinking about it, there's that withered bouquet of flowers in Mum's room. I should look at Sweetpea.
Sweetpea :
A present given upon departure !
&
Thistle :
Defiance.
She did leave me a message!
Okay, Mum. If we're playing it your way, then I know where your chrysanthemum is!
SLAM!

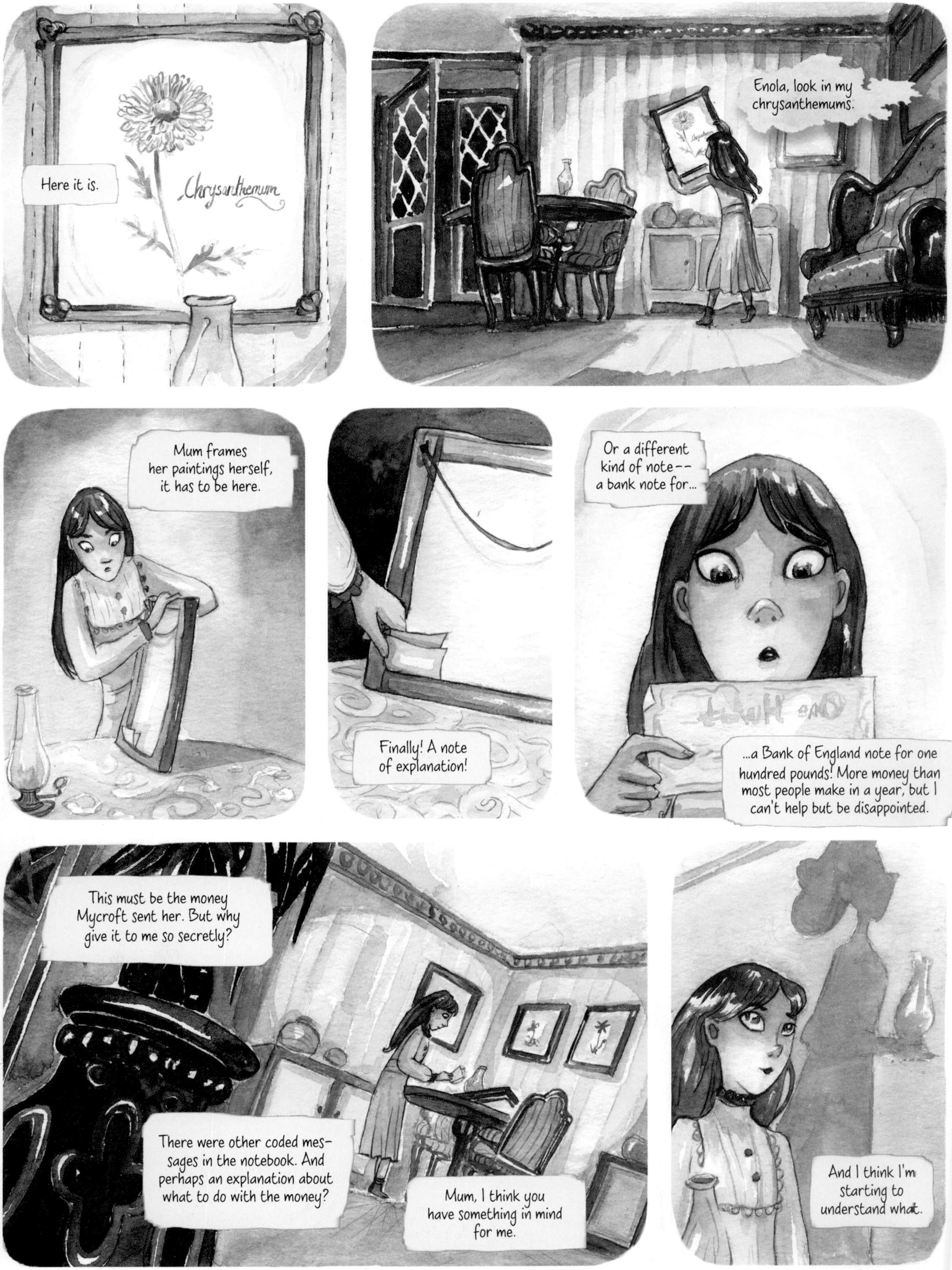
Here it is.
Chrysanthemum
Enola, look in my chrysanthemums.
Mum frames her paintings herself, it has to be here.
Finally! A note of explanation!
Or a different kind of note-- a bank note for...
...a Bank of England note for one hundred pounds! More money than most people make in a year, but I can't help but be disappointed.
This must be the money Mycroft sent her. But why give it to me so secretly?
There were other coded messages in the notebook. And perhaps an explanation about what to do with the money?
Mum, I think you have something in mind for me.
And I think I'm starting to understand what.

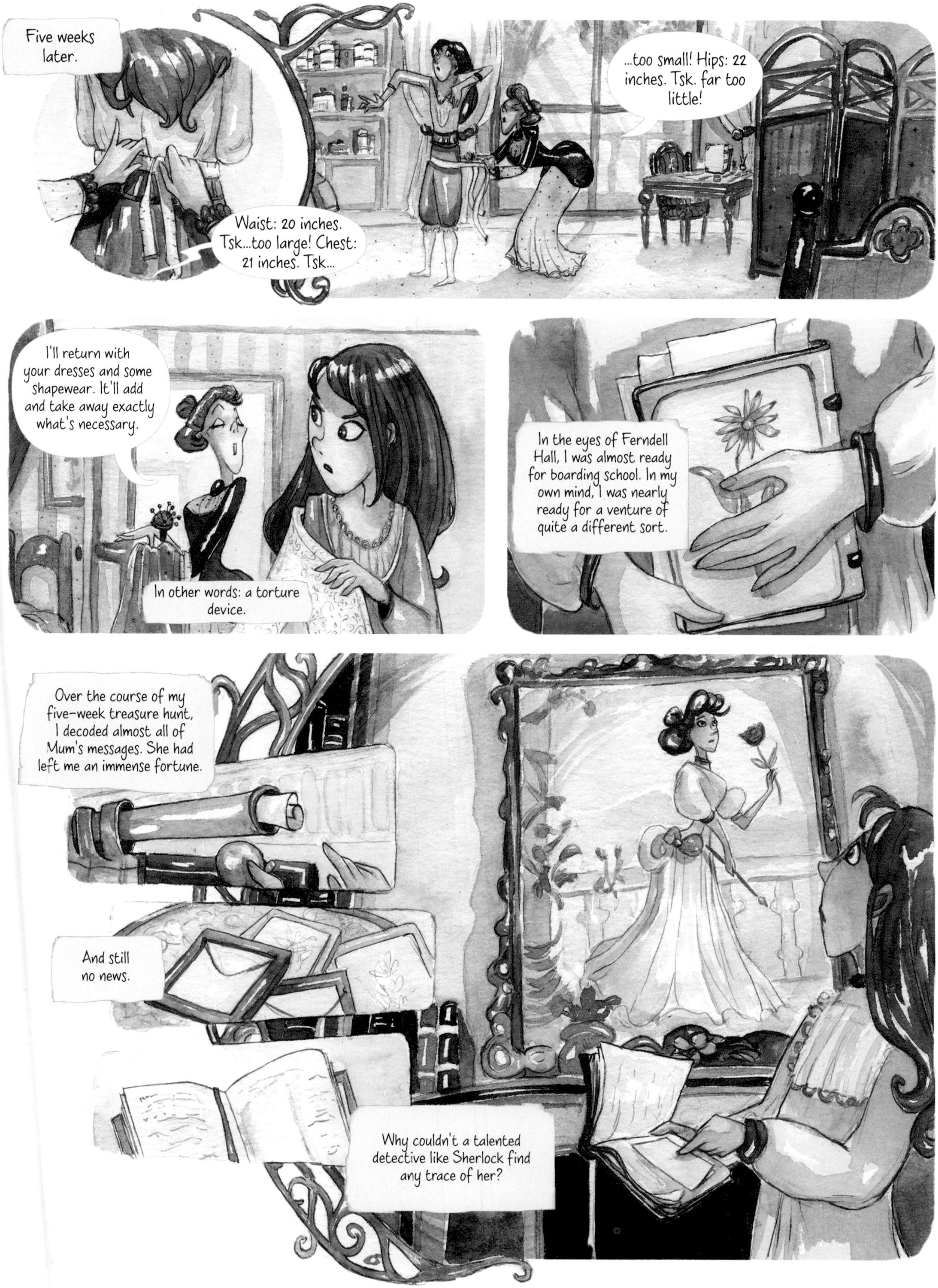
Five weeks later.
Waist: 20 inches. Tsk...too large! Chest: 21 inches. Tsk...
...too small! Hips: 22 inches. Tsk. far too little!
I'll return with your dresses and some shapewear. It'll add and take away exactly what's necessary.
In other words: a torture device.
In the eyes of Ferndell Hall, I was almost ready for boarding school. In my own mind, I was nearly ready for a venture of quite a different sort.
Over the course of my five-week treasure hunt, I decoded almost all of Mum's messages. She had left me an immense fortune.
And still no news.
Why couldn't a talented detective like Sherlock find any trace of her?

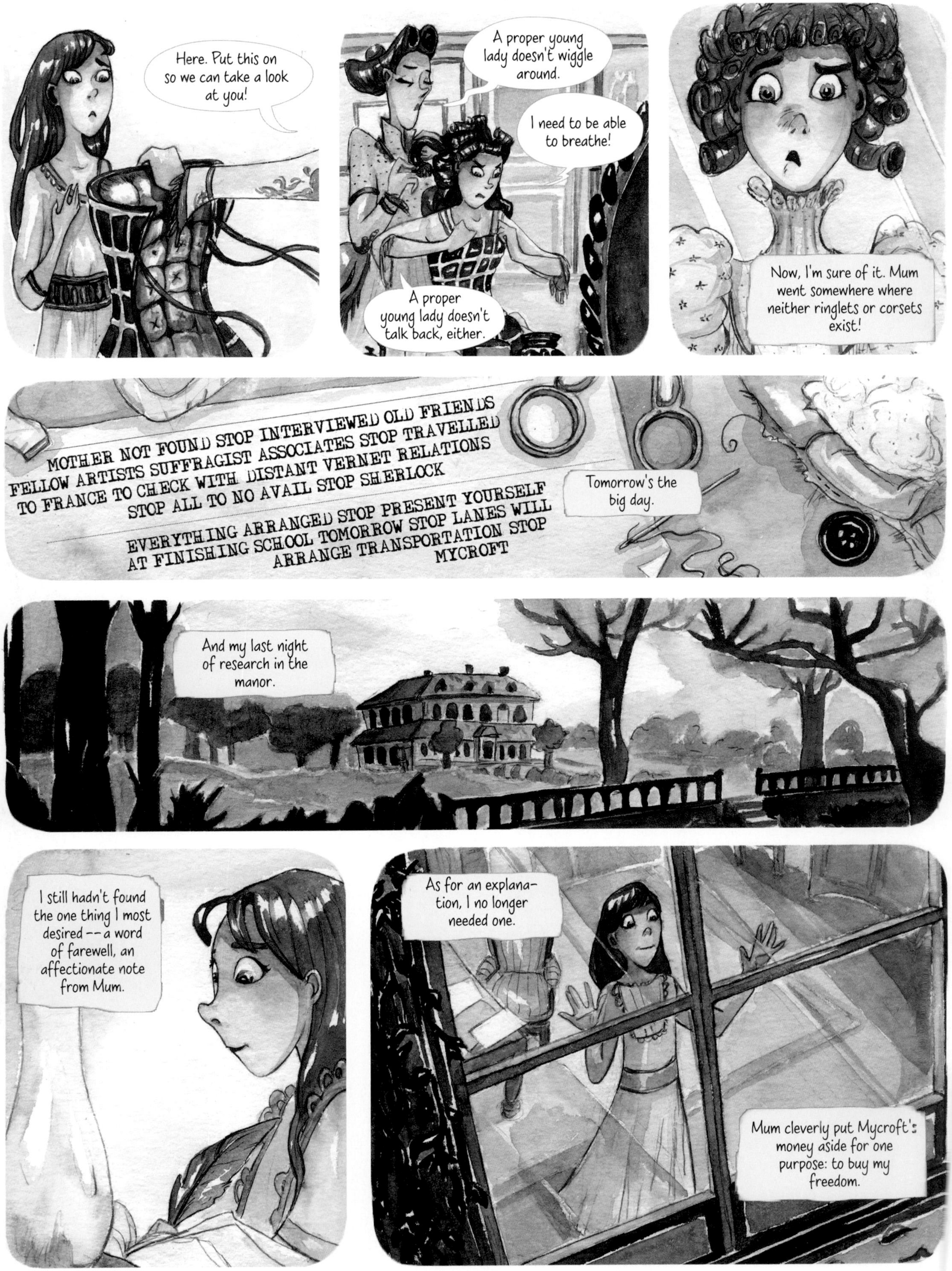
Here. Put this on so we can take a look at you!
A proper young lady doesn't wiggle around.
I need to be able to breathe!
A proper young lady doesn't talk back, either.
Now, I'm sure of it. Mum went somewhere where neither ringlets or corsets exist!
MOTHER NOT FOUND STOP INTERVIEWED OLD FRIENDS FELLOW ARTISTS SUFFRAGIST ASSOCIATES STOP TRAVELLED TO FRANCE TO CHECK WITH DISTANT VERNET RELATIONS STOP ALL TO NO AVAIL STOP SHERLOCK
EVERYTHING ARRANGED STOP PRESENT YOURSELF AT FINISHING SCHOOL TOMORROW STOP LANES WILL ARRANGE TRANSPORTATION STOP MYCROFT
Tomorrow's the big day.
And my last night of research in the manor.
I still hadn't found the one thing I most desired -- a word of farewell, an affectionate note from Mum.
As for an explanation, I no longer needed one.
Mum cleverly put Mycroft's money aside for one purpose: to buy my freedom.

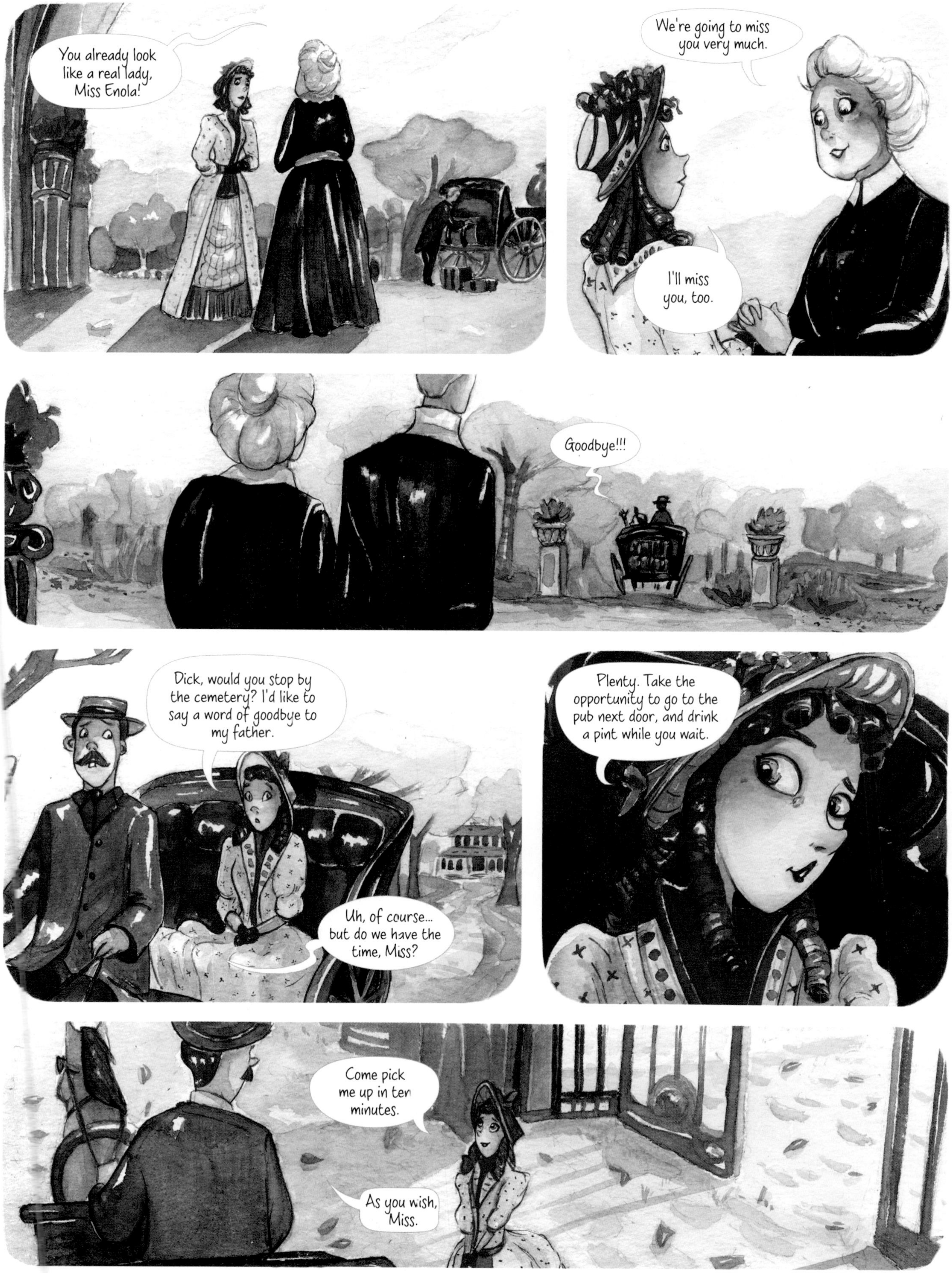

You already look like a real lady, Miss Enola!
We're going to miss you very much.
I'll miss you, too.
Goodbye!!!
Dick, would you stop by the cemetery? I'd like to say a word of goodbye to my father.
Uh, of course... but do we have the time, Miss?
Plenty. Take the opportunity to go to the pub next door, and drink a pint while you wait.
Come pick me up in ten minutes.
As you wish, Miss.

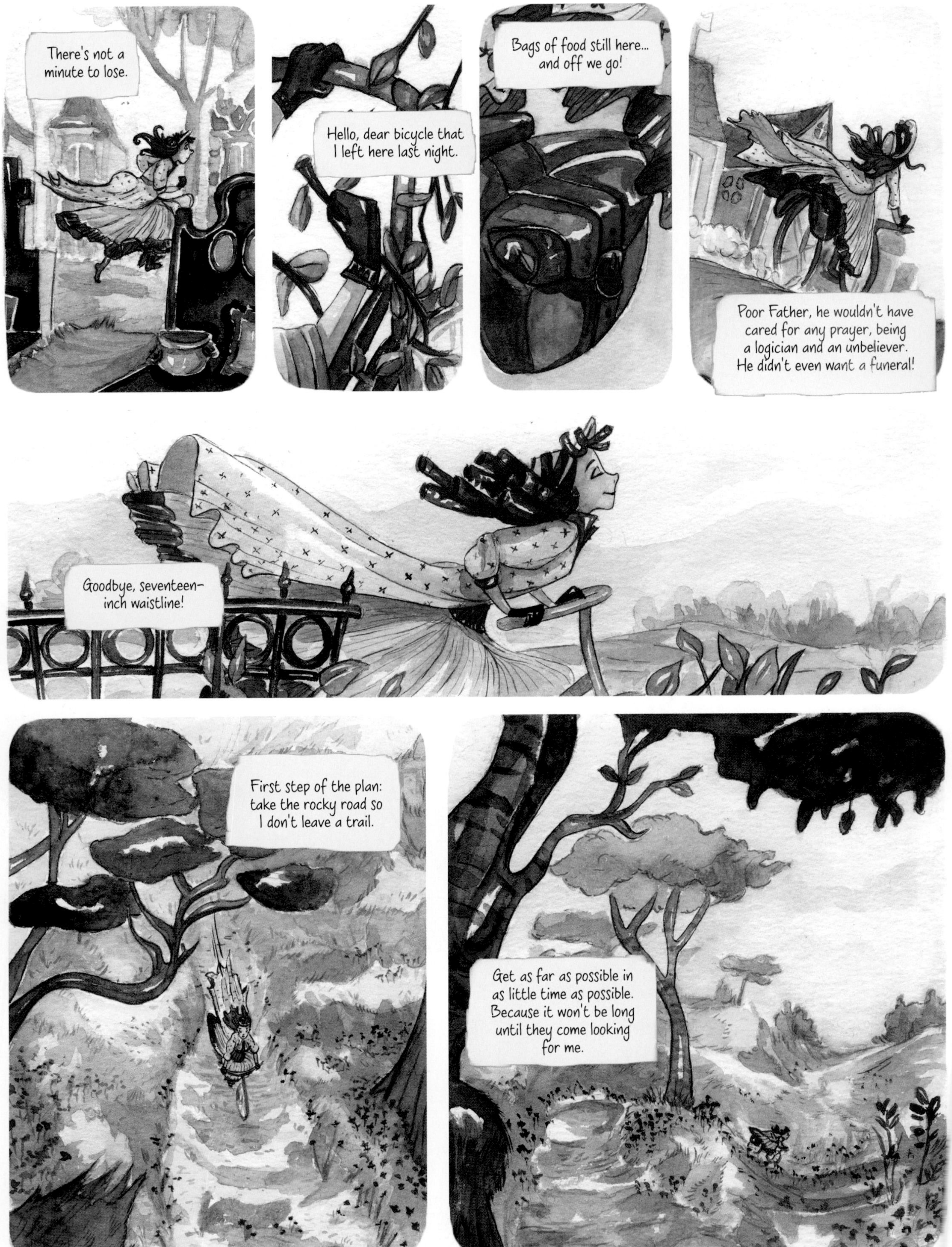
There's not a minute to lose.
Hello, dear bicycle that I left here last night.
Bags of food still here... and off we go!
Poor Father, he wouldn't have cared for any prayer, being a logician and an unbeliever. He didn't even want a funeral!
Goodbye, seventeen-inch waistline!
First step of the plan: take the rocky road so I don't leave a trail.
Get as far as possible in as little time as possible. Because it won't be long until they come looking for me.

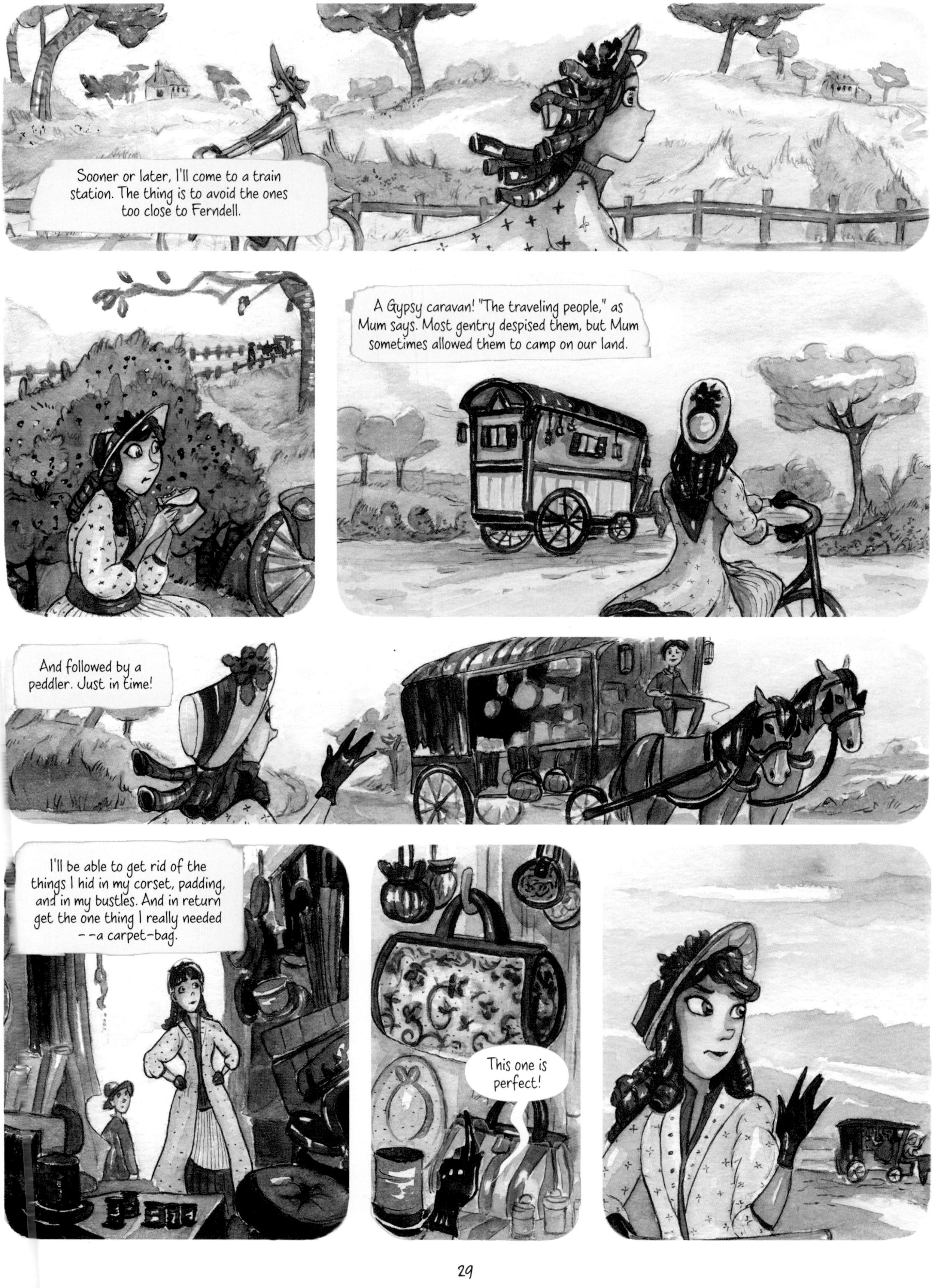
Sooner or later, I'll come to a train station. The thing is to avoid the ones too close to Ferndell.
A Gypsy caravan! "The traveling people," as Mum says. Most gentry despised them, but Mum sometimes allowed them to camp on our land.
And followed by a peddler. Just in time!
I'll be able to get rid of the things I hid in my corset, padding, and in my bustles. And in return get the one thing I really needed --a carpet-bag.
This one is perfect!

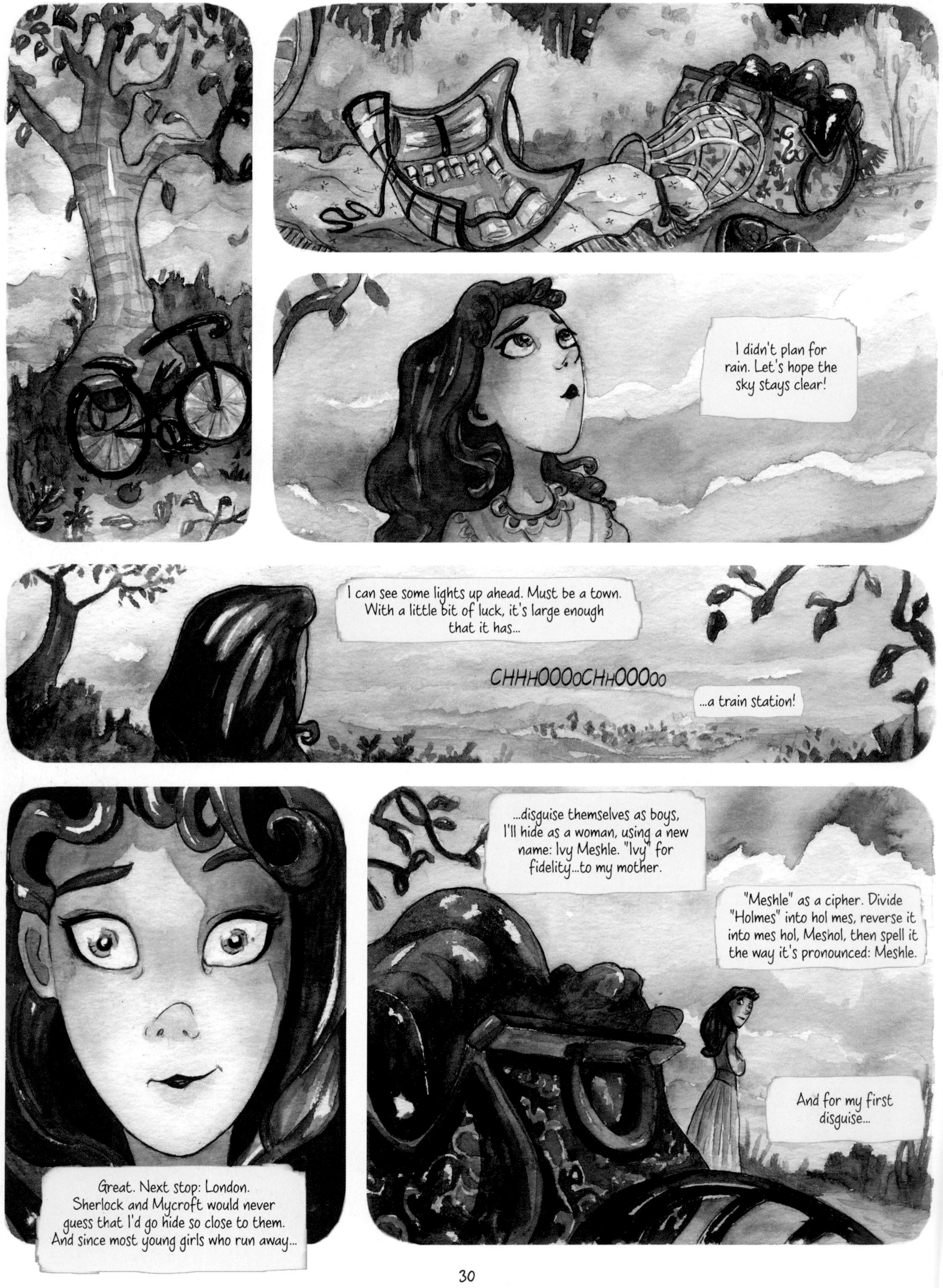
I didn't plan for rain. Let's hope the sky stays clear!
I can see some lights up ahead. Must be a town. With a little bit of luck, it's large enough that it has...
CHHHOOOoCHHOOOoo
...a train station!
Great. Next stop: London. Sherlock and Mycroft would never guess that I'd go hide so close to them. And since most young girls who run away...
...disguise themselves as boys, I'll hide as a woman, using a new name: Ivy Meshle. "Ivy" for fidelity...to my mother.
"Meshle" as a cipher. Divide "Holmes" into hol mes, reverse it into mes hol, Meshol, then spell it the way it's pronounced: Meshle.
And for my first disguise...

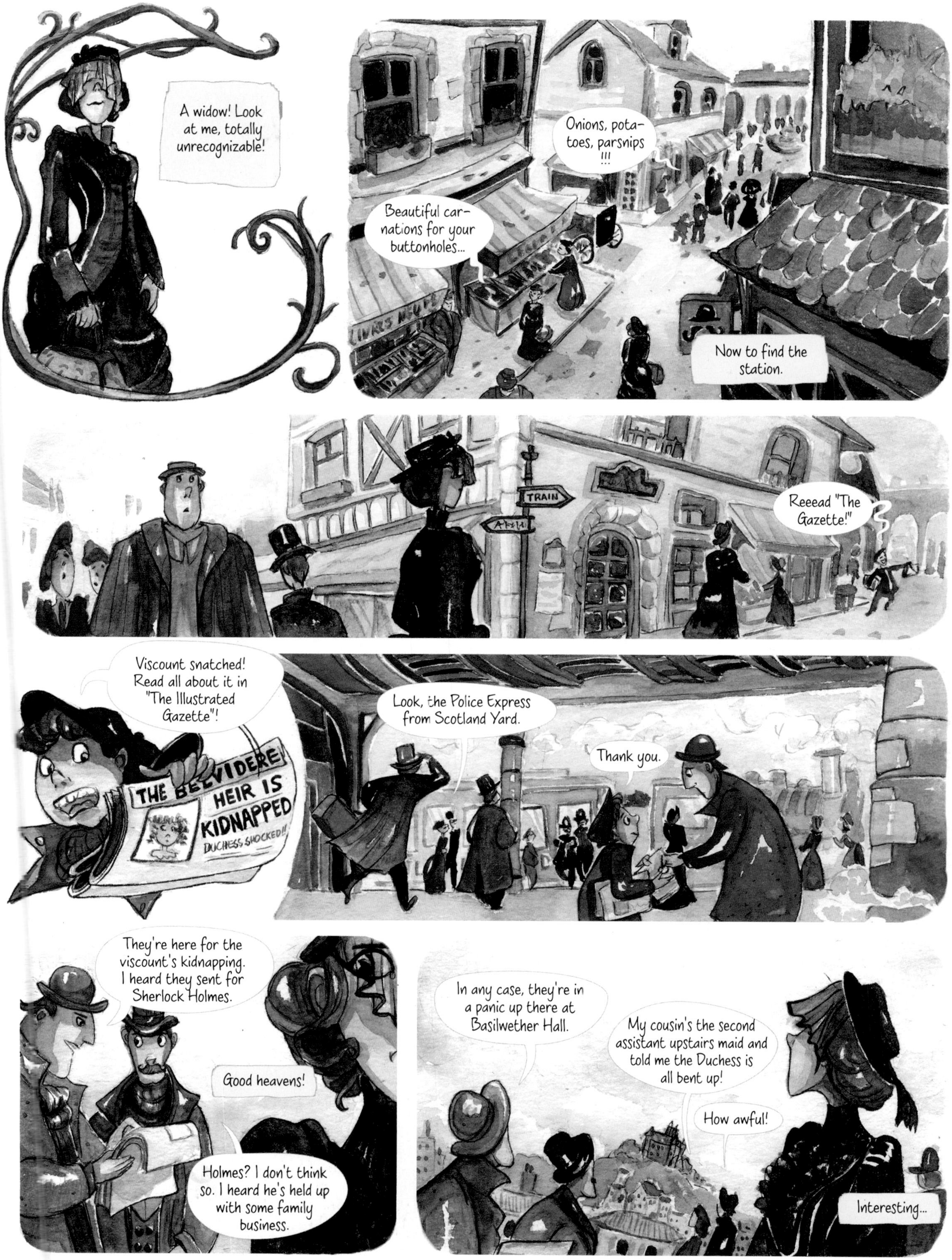
A widow! Look at me, totally unrecognizable!
Onions, potatoes, parsnips !!!
Beautiful carnations for your buttonholes...
Now to find the station.
TRAIN
Reeead "The Gazette!"
Viscount snatched! Read all about it in "The Illustrated Gazette"!
THE BELVIDERE HEIR IS KIDNAPPED
DUCHESS SHOCKED!!
Look, the Police Express from Scotland Yard.
Thank you.
They're here for the viscount's kidnapping. I heard they sent for Sherlock Holmes.
Good heavens!
Holmes? I don't think so. I heard he's held up with some family business.
In any case, they're in a panic up there at Basilwether Hall.
My cousin's the second assistant upstairs maid and told me the Duchess is all bent up!
How awful!
Interesting...

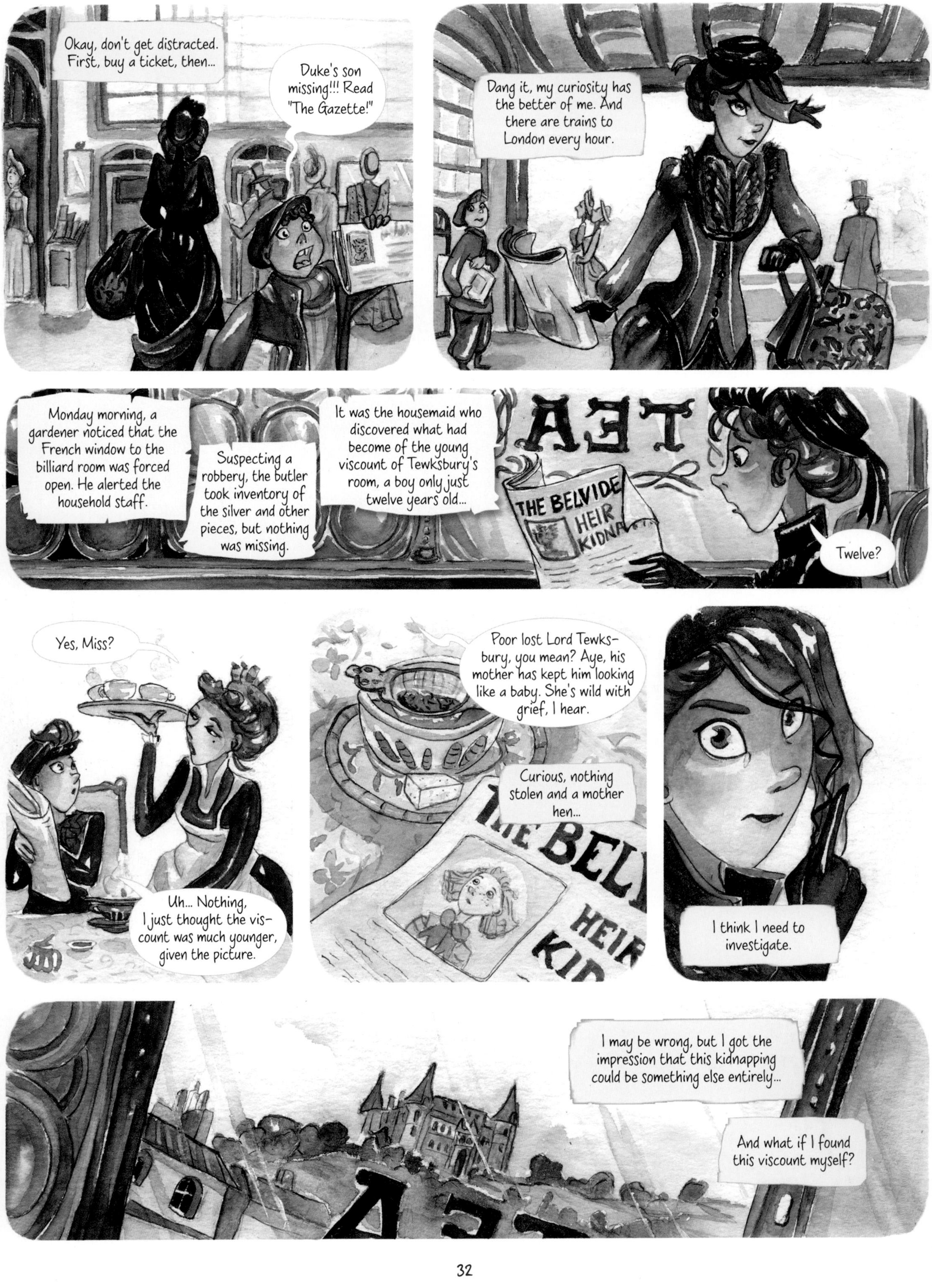

Okay, don't get distracted. First, buy a ticket, then...
Duke's son missing!!! Read "The Gazette!"
Dang it, my curiosity has the better of me. And there are trains to London every hour.
Monday morning, a gardener noticed that the French window to the billiard room was forced open. He alerted the household staff.
Suspecting a robbery, the butler took inventory of the silver and other pieces, but nothing was missing.
It was the housemaid who discovered what had become of the young viscount of Tewksbury's room, a boy only just twelve years old...
TEA
THE BELVIDE
HEIR KIDNA
Twelve?
Yes, Miss?
Uh... Nothing, I just thought the vis-count was much younger, given the picture.
Poor lost Lord Tewks-bury, you mean? Aye, his mother has kept him looking like a baby. She's wild with grief, I hear.
Curious, nothing stolen and a mother hen...
THE BEL
HEIR KID
I think I need to investigate.
I may be wrong, but I got the impression that this kidnapping could be something else entirely...
And what if I found this viscount myself?

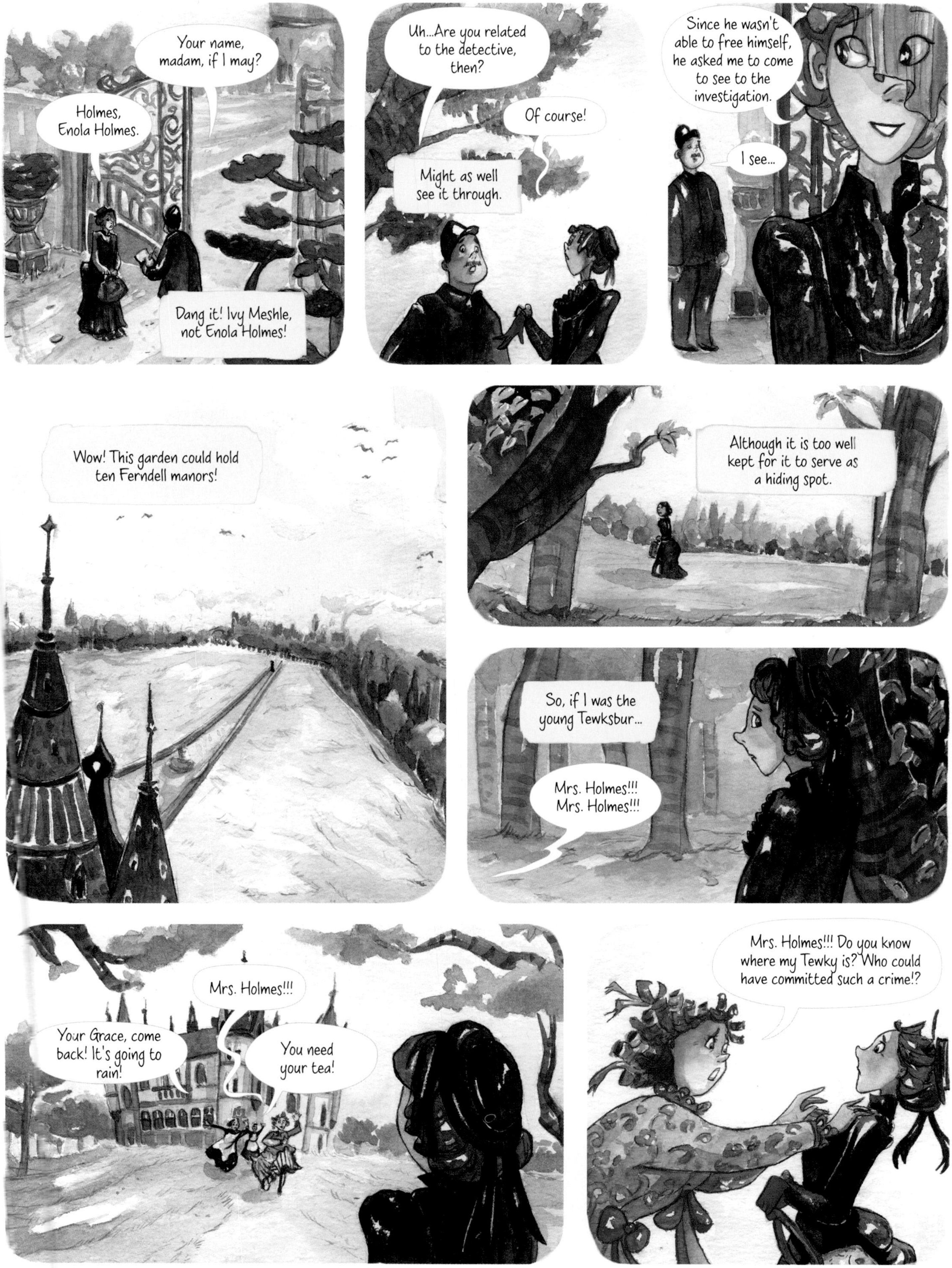
Your name, madam, if I may?
Holmes, Enola Holmes.
Dang it! Ivy Meshle, not Enola Holmes!
Uh...Are you related to the detective, then?
Of course!
Might as well see it through.
Since he wasn't able to free himself, he asked me to come to see to the investigation.
I see...
Wow! This garden could hold ten Ferndell manors!
Although it is too well kept for it to serve as a hiding spot.
So, if I was the young Tewksbur...
Mrs. Holmes!!! Mrs. Holmes!!!
Your Grace, come back! It's going to rain!
Mrs. Holmes!!!
You need your tea!
Mrs. Holmes!!! Do you know where my Tewky is? Who could have committed such a crime!?

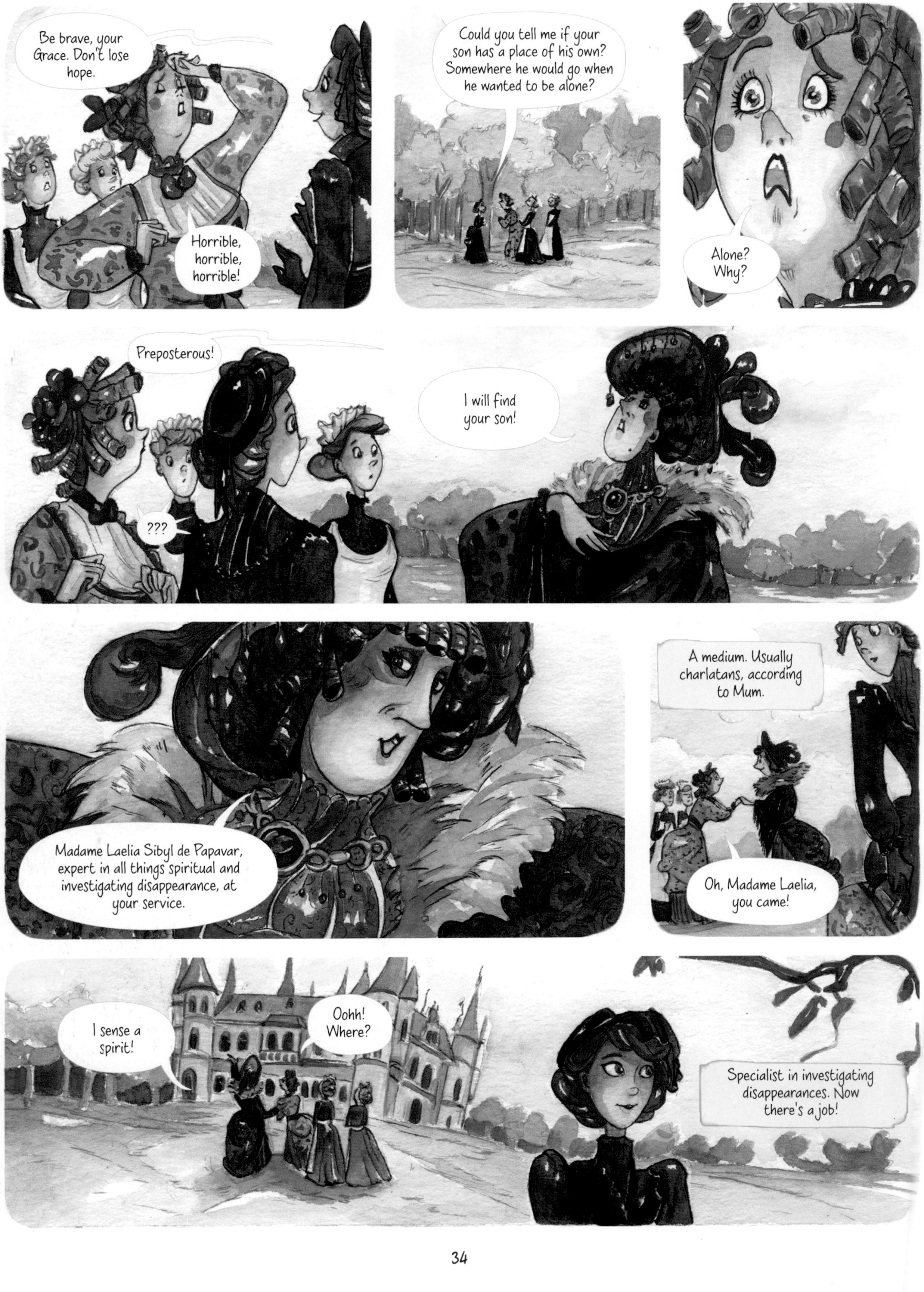

Be brave, your Grace. Don't lose hope.
Horrible, horrible, horrible!
Could you tell me if your son has a place of his own? Somewhere he would go when he wanted to be alone?
Alone? Why?
Preposterous!
???
I will find your son!
Madame Laelia Sibyl de Papavar, expert in all things spiritual and investigating disappearance, at your service.
A medium. Usually charlatans, according to Mum.
Oh, Madame Laelia, you came!
I sense a spirit!
Oohh! Where?
Specialist in investigating disappearances. Now there's a job!

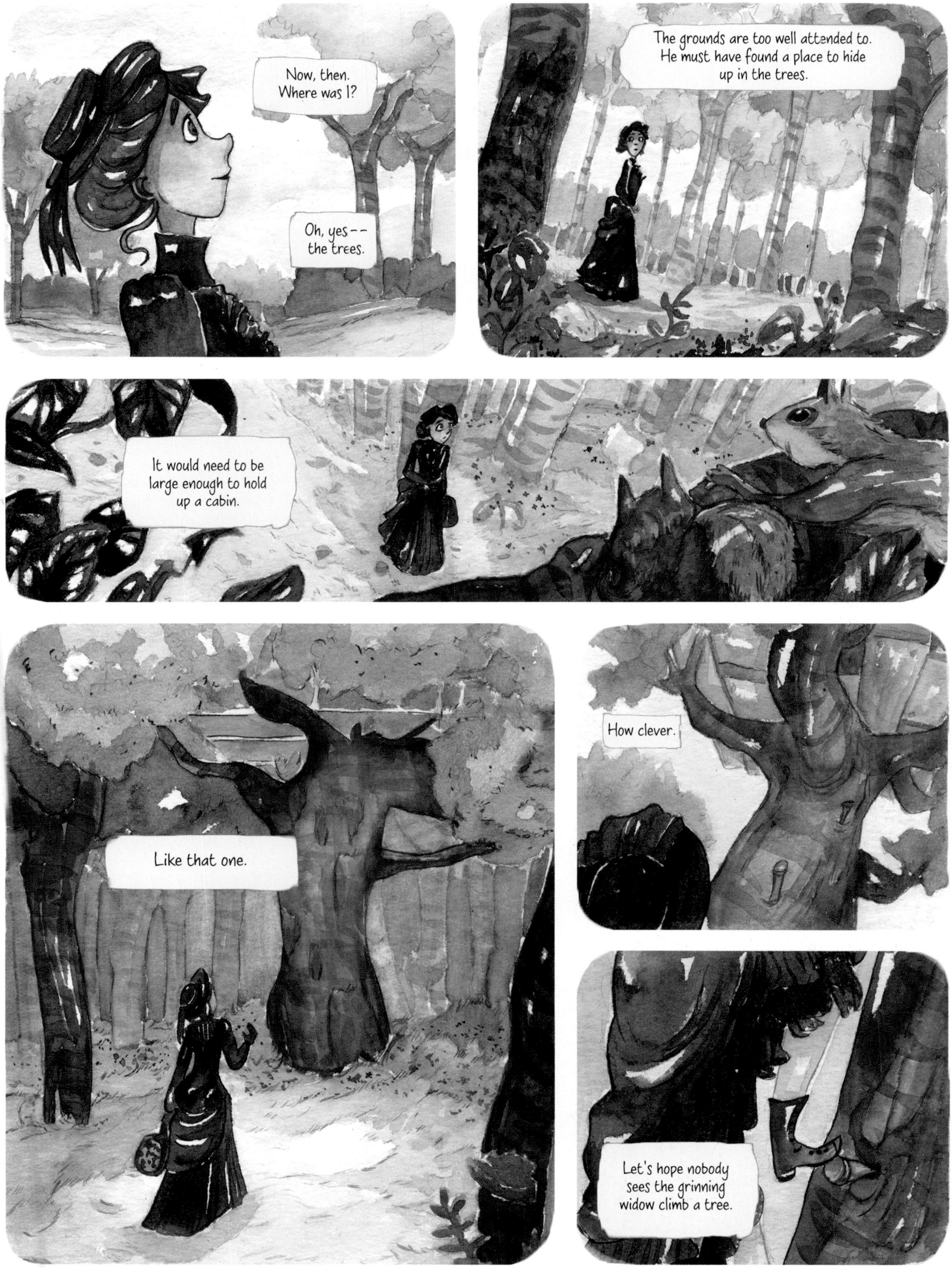
Now, then.
Where was I?
Oh, yes--
the trees.
The grounds are too well attended to.
He must have found a place to hide
up in the trees.
It would need to be
large enough to hold
up a cabin.
Like that one.
How clever.
Let's hope nobody
sees the grinning
widow climb a tree.

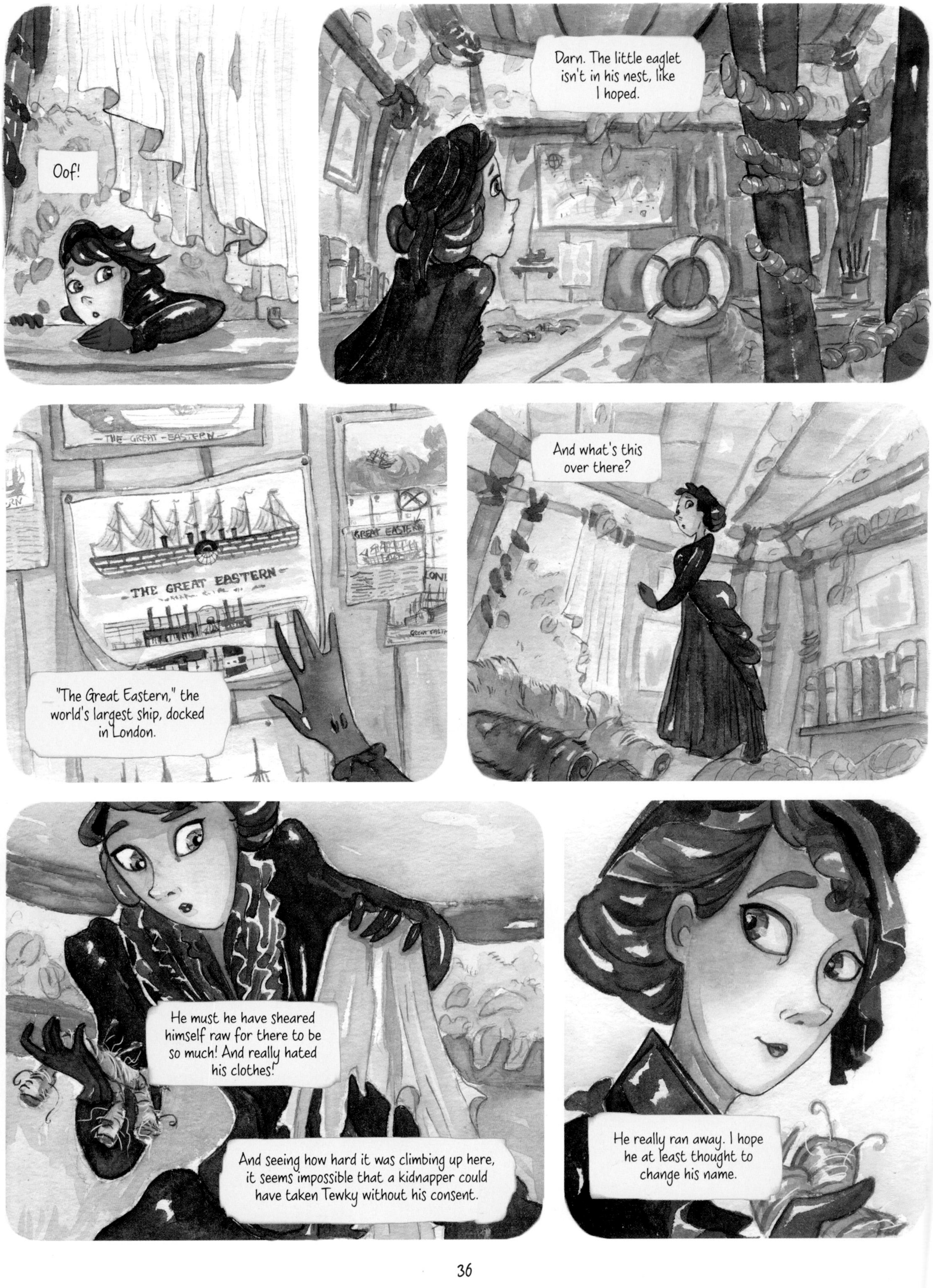
Oof!
Darn. The little eaglet isn't in his nest, like I hoped.
THE GREAT EASTERN
THE GREAT EASTERN
GREAT EASTERN
"The Great Eastern," the world's largest ship, docked in London.
And what's this over there?
He must he have sheared himself raw for there to be so much! And really hated his clothes!
And seeing how hard it was climbing up here, it seems impossible that a kidnapper could have taken Tewky without his consent.
He really ran away. I hope he at least thought to change his name.

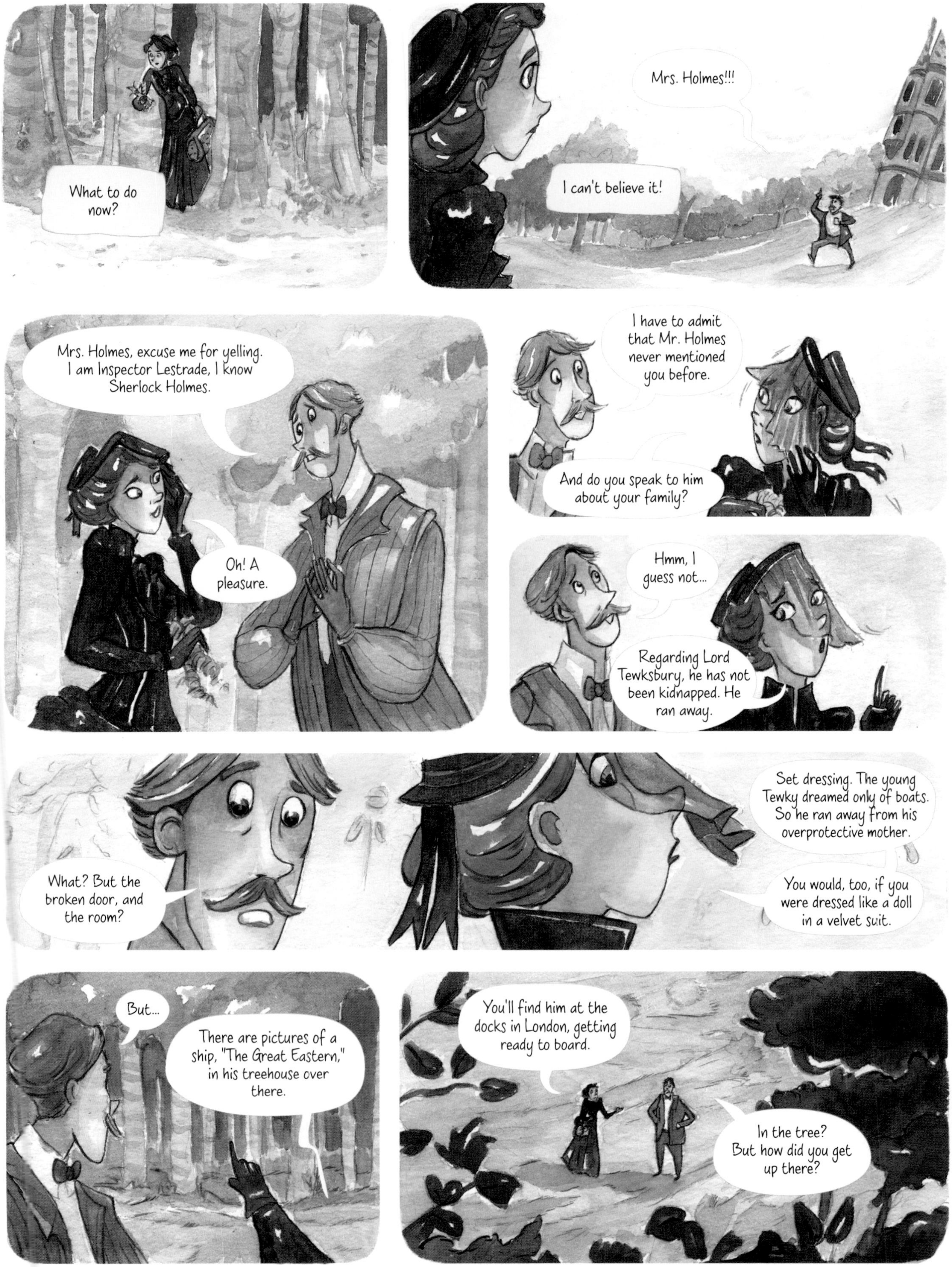
What to do now?
Mrs. Holmes!!!
I can't believe it!
Mrs. Holmes, excuse me for yelling. I am Inspector Lestrade, I know Sherlock Holmes.
Oh! A pleasure.
I have to admit that Mr. Holmes never mentioned you before.
And do you speak to him about your family?
Hmm, I guess not...
Regarding Lord Tewksbury, he has not been kidnapped. He ran away.
What? But the broken door, and the room?
Set dressing. The young Tewky dreamed only of boats. So he ran away from his overprotective mother.
You would, too, if you were dressed like a doll in a velvet suit.
But...
There are pictures of a ship, "The Great Eastern," in his treehouse over there.
You'll find him at the docks in London, getting ready to board.
In the tree? But how did you get up there?

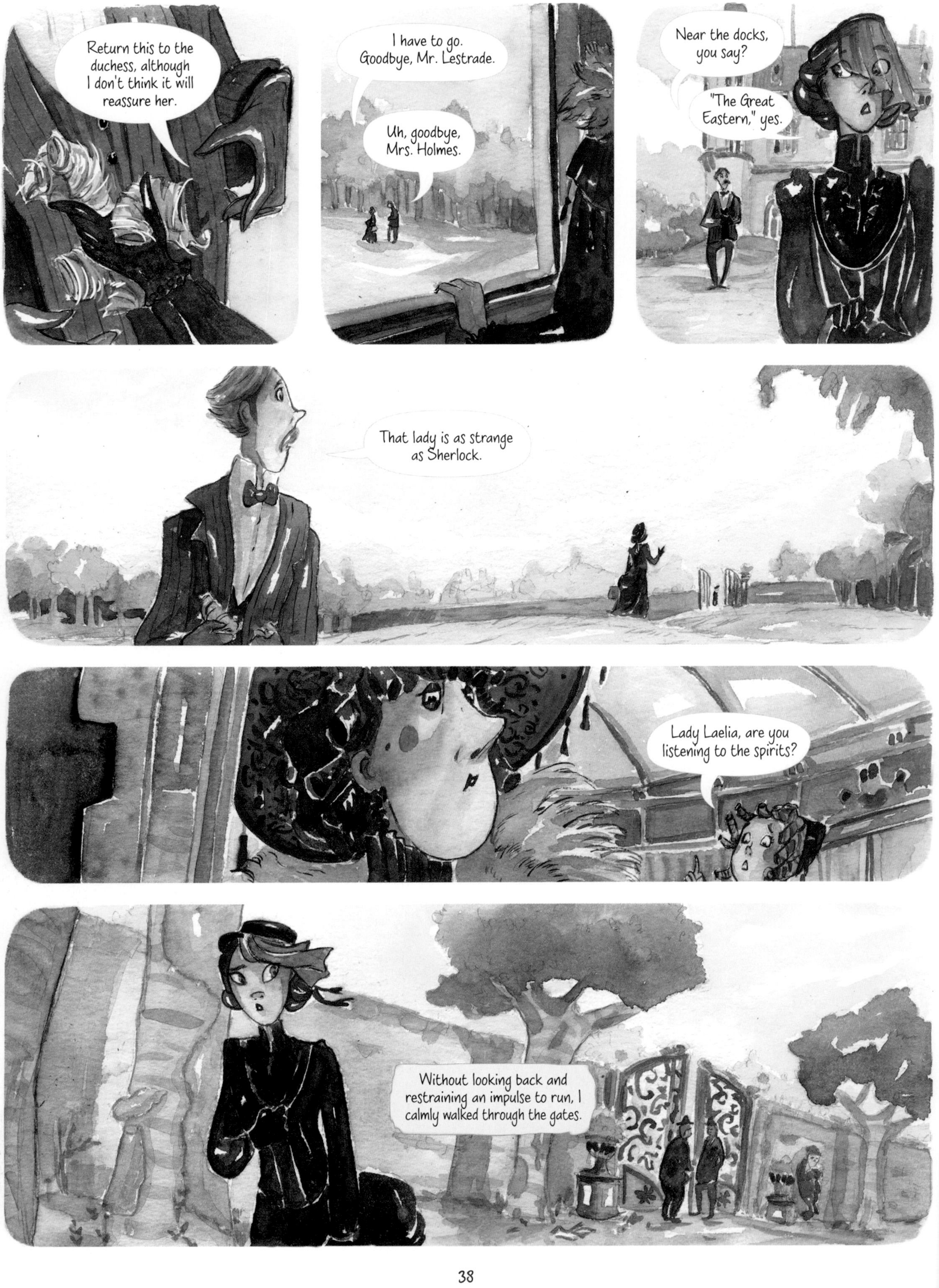
Return this to the duchess, although I don't think it will reassure her.
I have to go. Goodbye, Mr. Lestrade.
Uh, goodbye, Mrs. Holmes.
Near the docks, you say?
"The Great Eastern," yes.
That lady is as strange as Sherlock.
Lady Laelia, are you listening to the spirits?
Without looking back and restraining an impulse to run, I calmly walked through the gates.

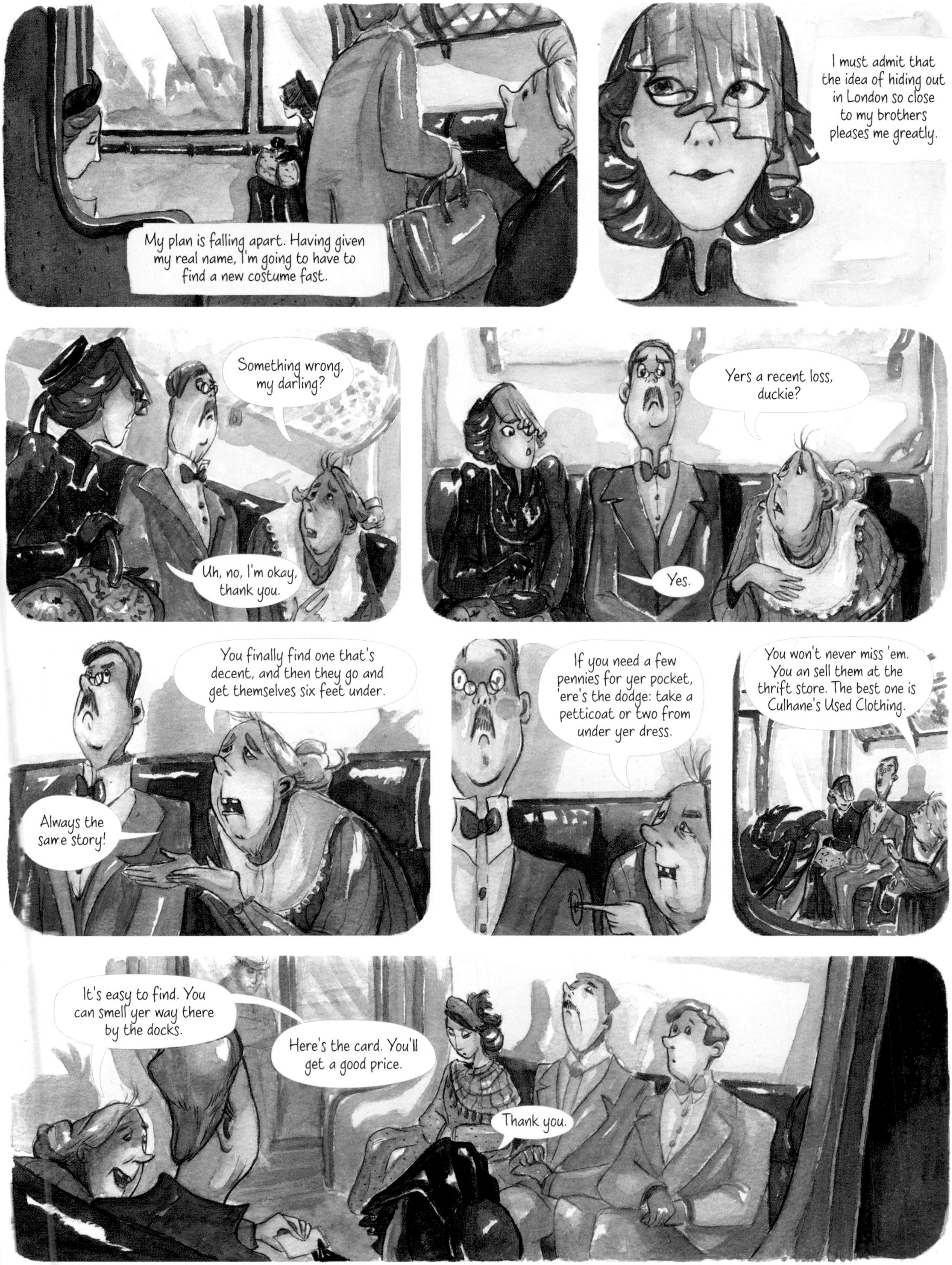
My plan is falling apart. Having given my real name, I'm going to have to find a new costume fast.
I must admit that the idea of hiding out in London so close to my brothers pleases me greatly.
Something wrong, my darling?
Uh, no, I'm okay, thank you.
Yers a recent loss, duckie?
Yes.
You finally find one that's decent, and then they go and get themselves six feet under.
Always the same story!
If you need a few pennies for yer pocket, 'ere's the dodge: take a petticoat or two from under yer dress.
You won't never miss 'em. You an sell them at the thrift store. The best one is Culhane's Used Clothing.
It's easy to find. You can smell yer way there by the docks.
Here's the card. You'll get a good price.
Thank you.

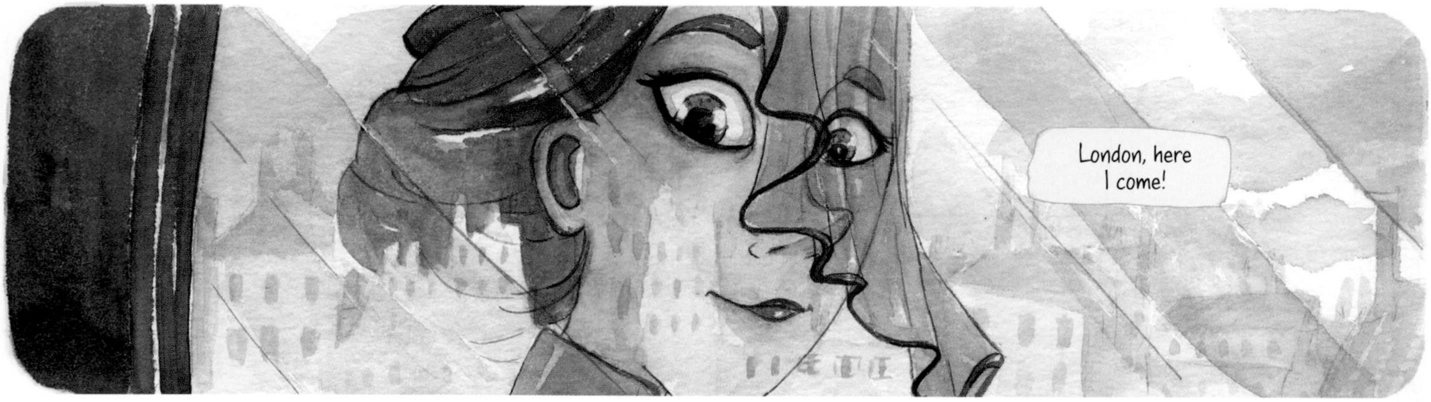
London, here
I come!

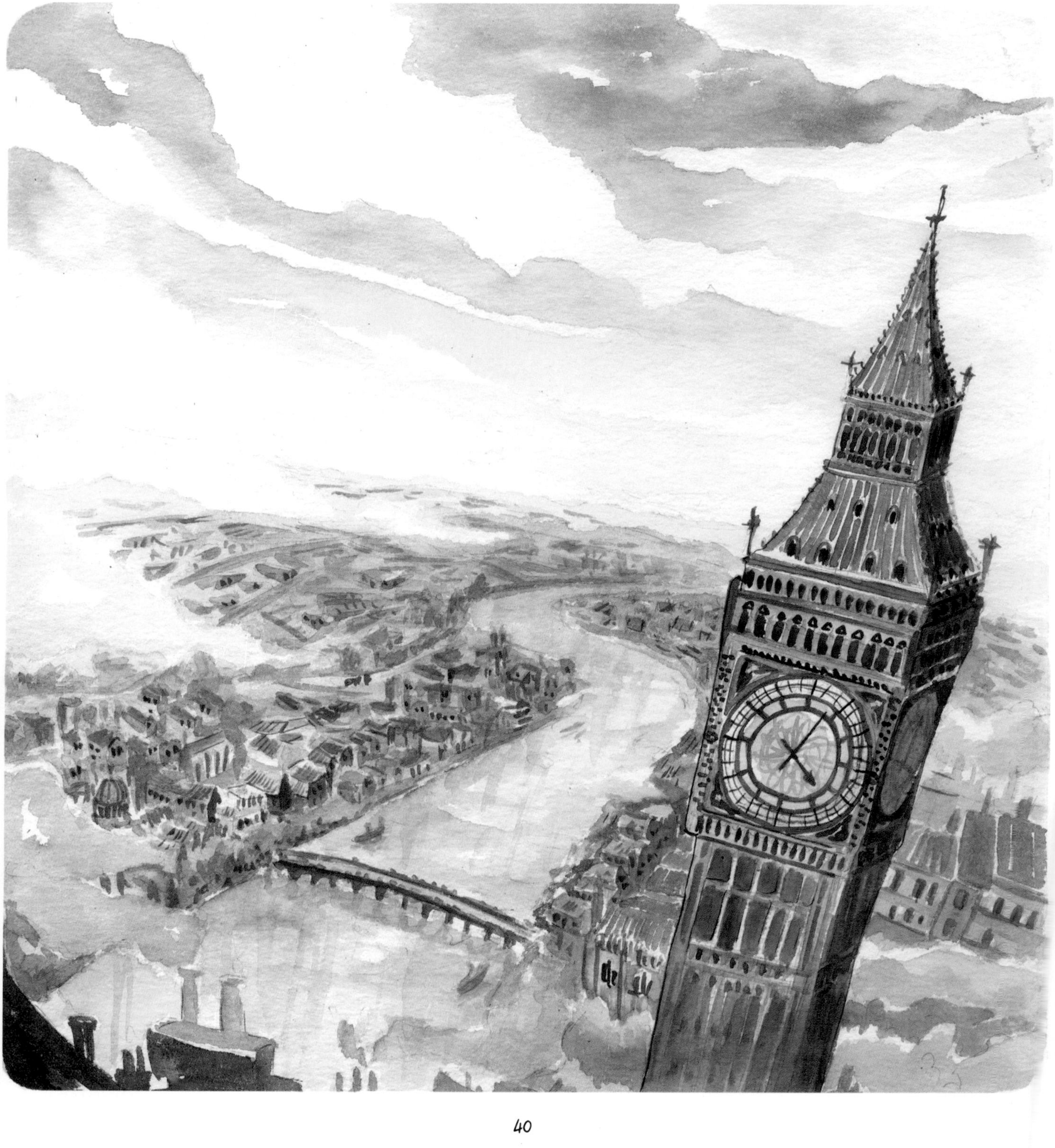

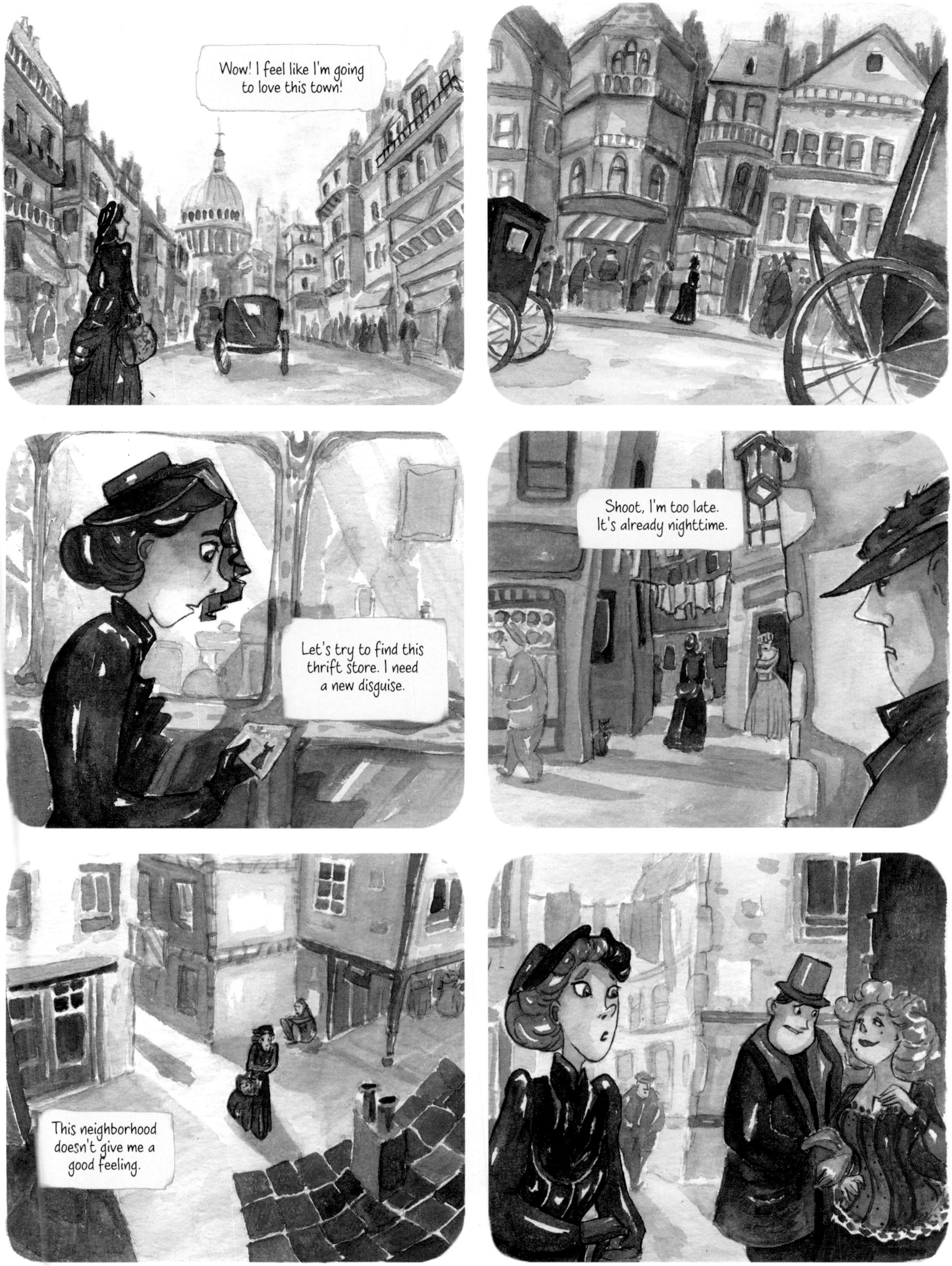
Wow! I feel like I'm going to love this town!
Let's try to find this thrift store. I need a new disguise.
Shoot, I'm too late. It's already nighttime.
This neighborhood doesn't give me a good feeling.

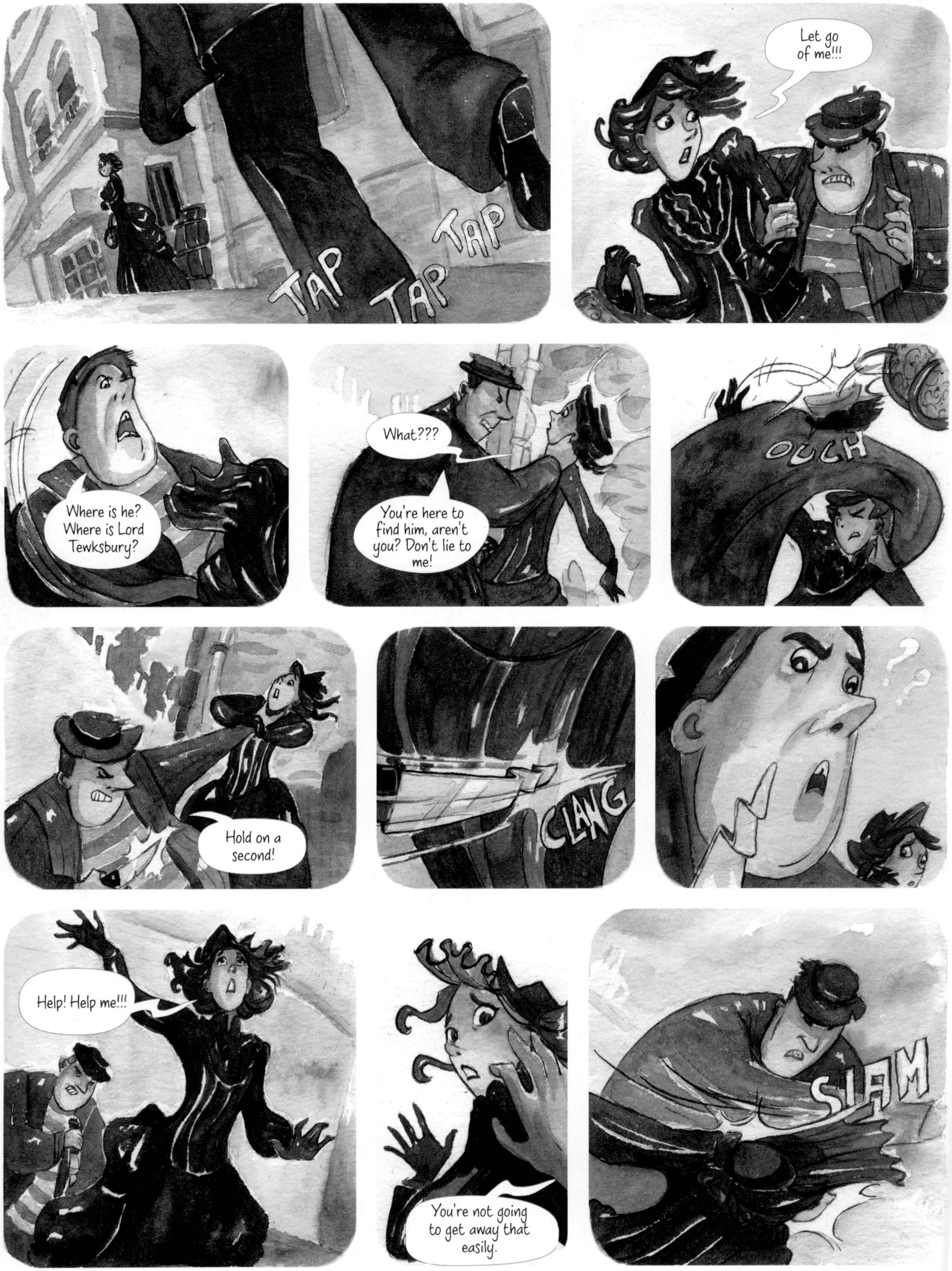
TAP
TAP
TAP
Let go of me!!!
Where is he? Where is Lord Tewksbury?
What???
You're here to find him, aren't you? Don't lie to me!
OUCH
Hold on a second!
CLANG
Help! Help me!!!
You're not going to get away that easily.
SLAM

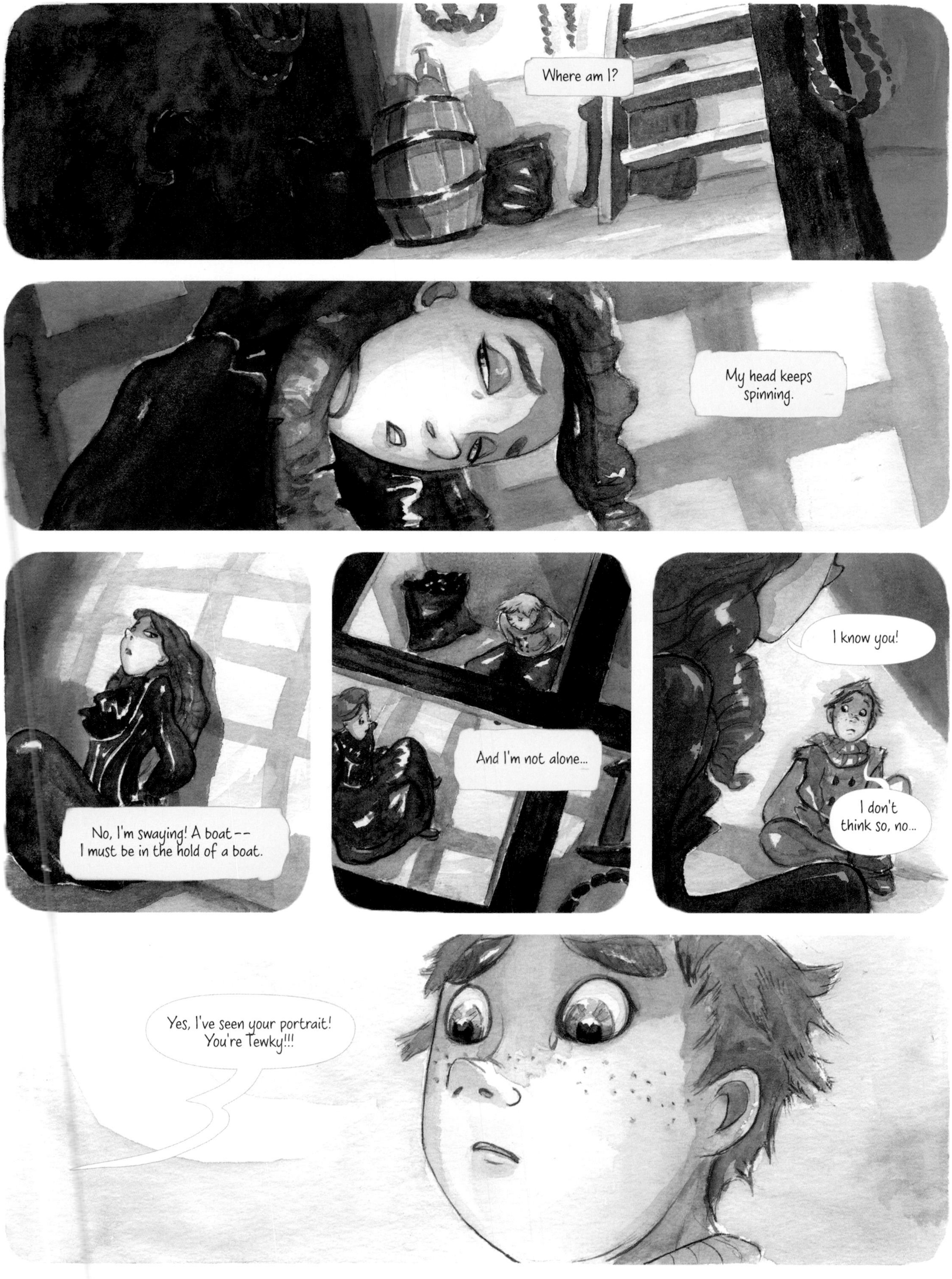
Where am I?
My head keeps spinning.
No, I'm swaying! A boat-- I must be in the hold of a boat.
And I'm not alone...
I know you!
I don't think so, no...
Yes, I've seen your portrait! You're Tewky!!!

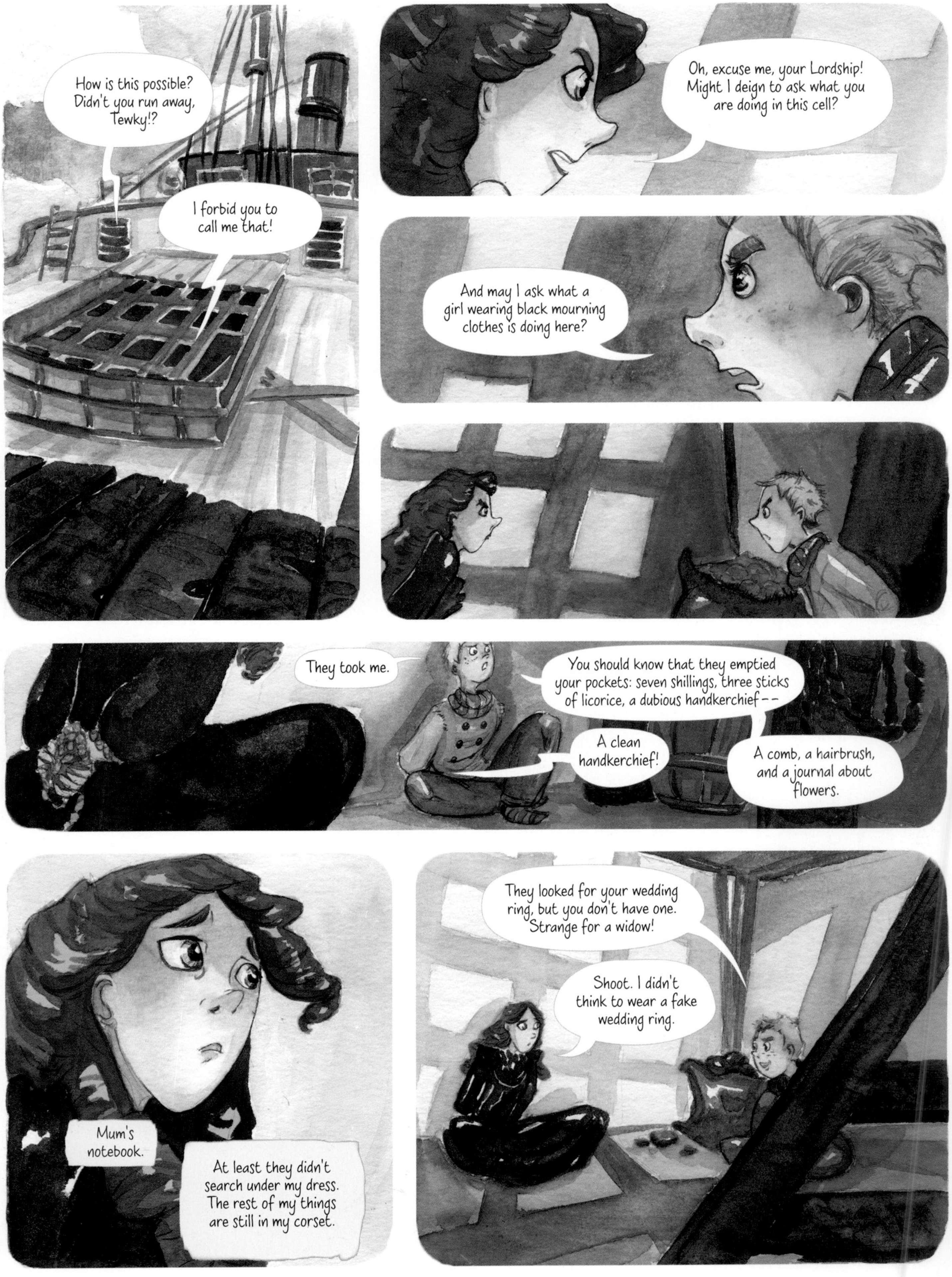
How is this possible? Didn't you run away, Tewky!?
I forbid you to call me that!
Oh, excuse me, your Lordship! Might I deign to ask what you are doing in this cell?
And may I ask what a girl wearing black mourning clothes is doing here?
They took me.
You should know that they emptied your pockets: seven shillings, three sticks of licorice, a dubious handkerchief--
A clean handkerchief!
A comb, a hairbrush, and a journal about flowers.
Mum's notebook.
At least they didn't search under my dress. The rest of my things are still in my corset.
They looked for your wedding ring, but you don't have one. Strange for a widow!
Shoot. I didn't think to wear a fake wedding ring.

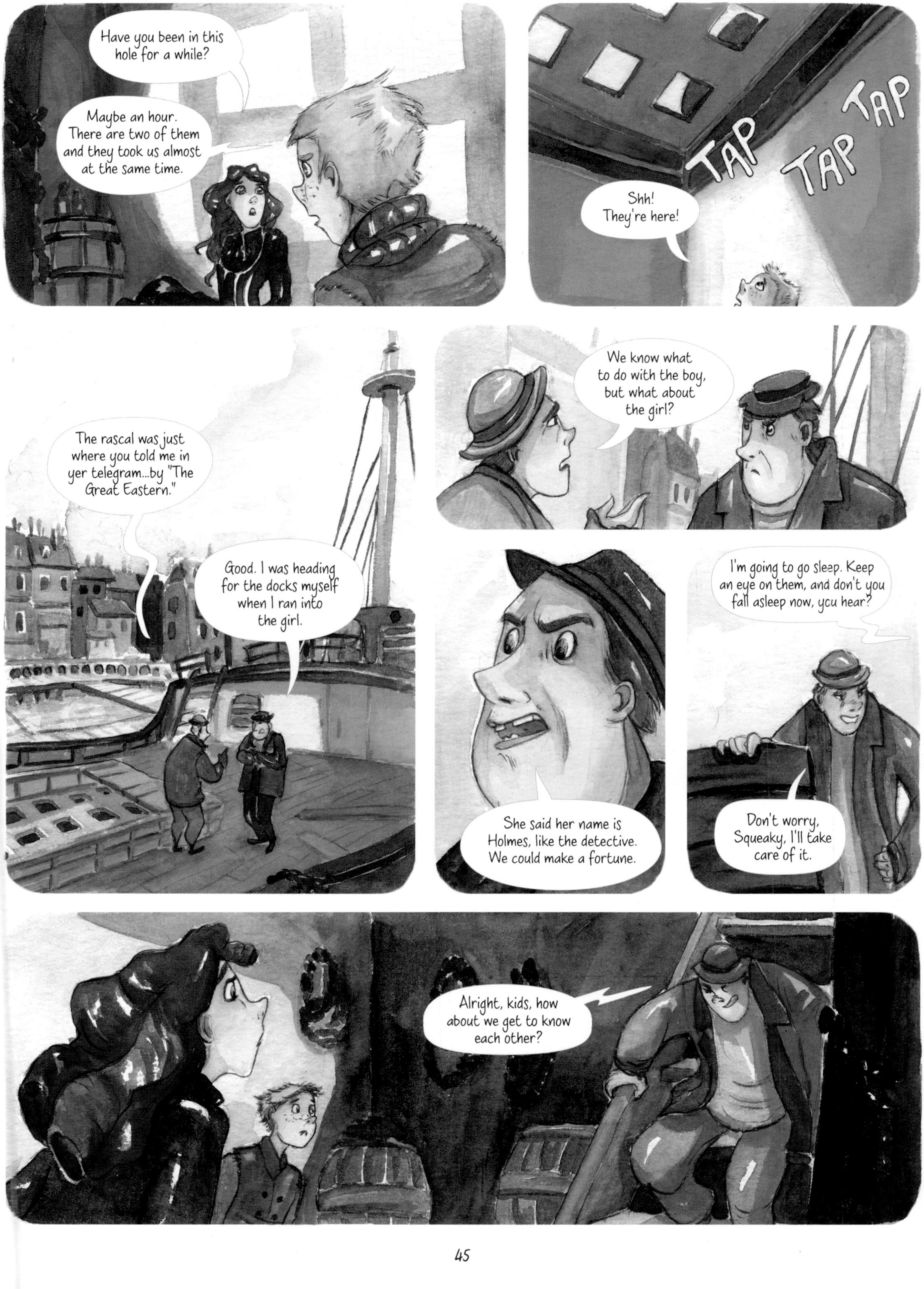
Have you been in this hole for a while?
Maybe an hour. There are two of them and they took us almost at the same time.
TAP TAP TAP
Shh! They're here!
The rascal was just where you told me in yer telegram...by "The Great Eastern."
Good. I was heading for the docks myself when I ran into the girl.
We know what to do with the boy, but what about the girl?
She said her name is Holmes, like the detective. We could make a fortune.
I'm going to go sleep. Keep an eye on them, and don't you fall asleep now, you hear?
Don't worry, Squeaky, I'll take care of it.
Alright, kids, how about we get to know each other?

What are you doing?

ZzzZZzzzzzz

If I can get one of the whalebones out of my corset, I could try to cut the rope...

There, I've got it. But it's going to take a little more time.

Hey! You!!!

Stop that!

Stop rockin' the boat!

No!

Make me! I desire this boat to rock. I command it!

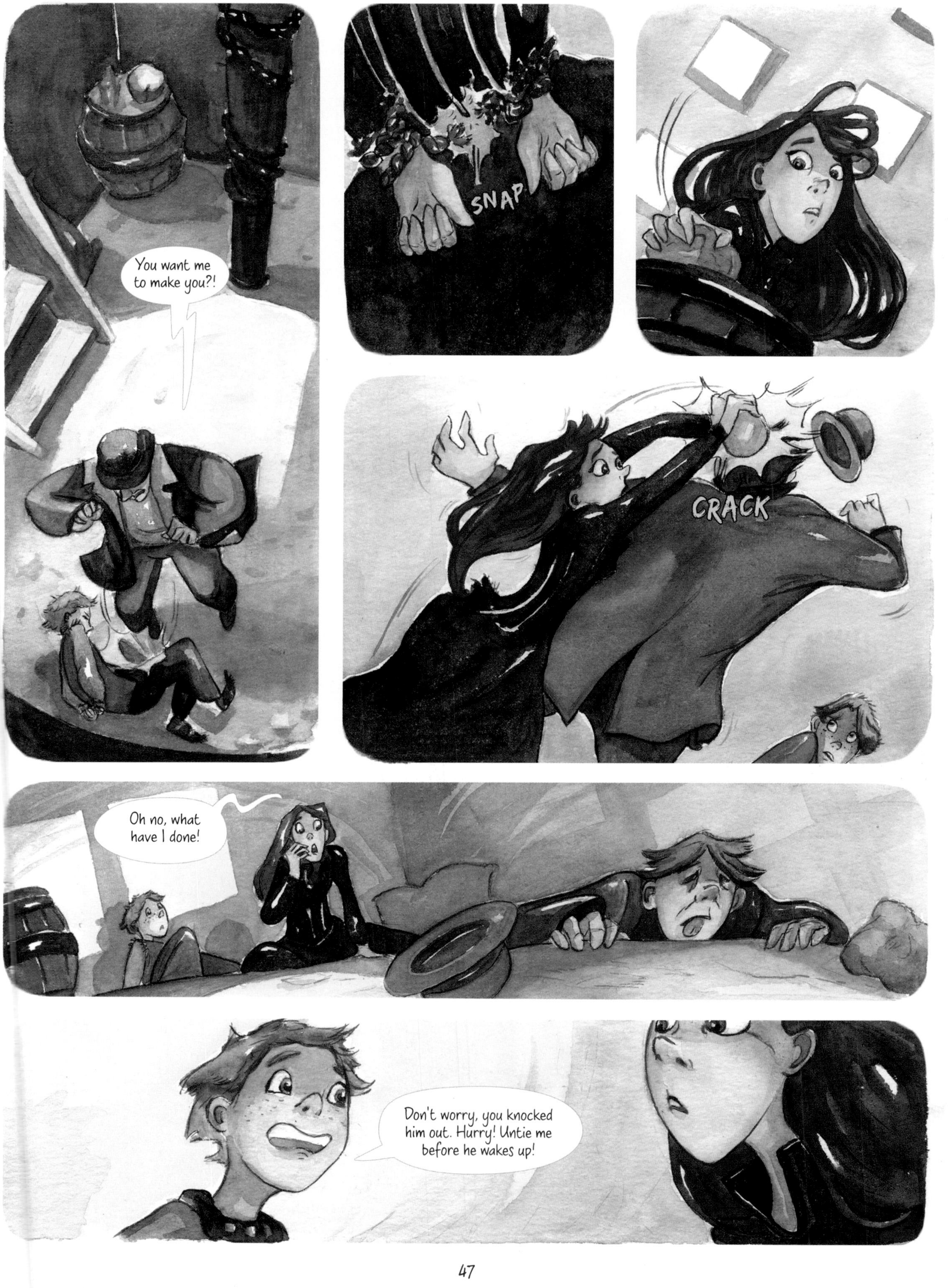

You want me to make you?!
SNAP
CRACK
Oh no, what have I done!
Don't worry, you knocked him out. Hurry! Untie me before he wakes up!

Hey! You there!
Quick!
Damn it, Cutter, what were you doing?! Catch them!!!
We need to find some place to hide!
There! At Culhane's!
CULHANE'S
You think she'll help us!?
If we pay her, she just might!
?!?

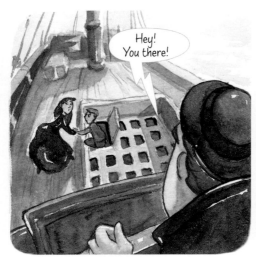

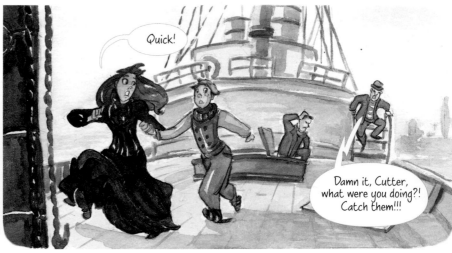

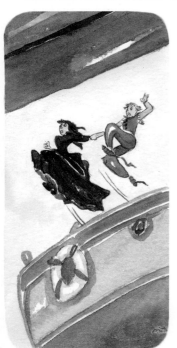

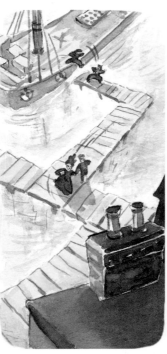

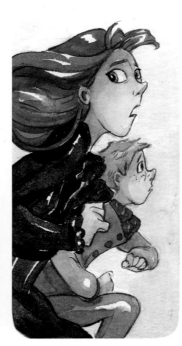

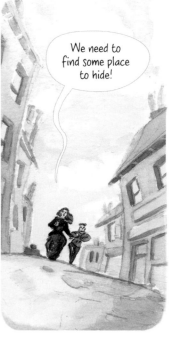

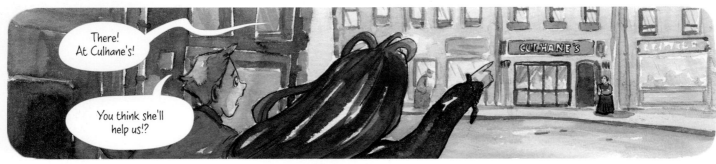

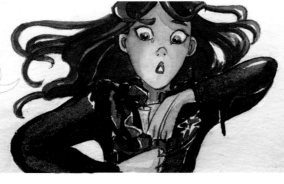

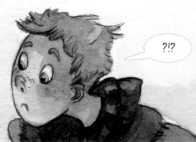

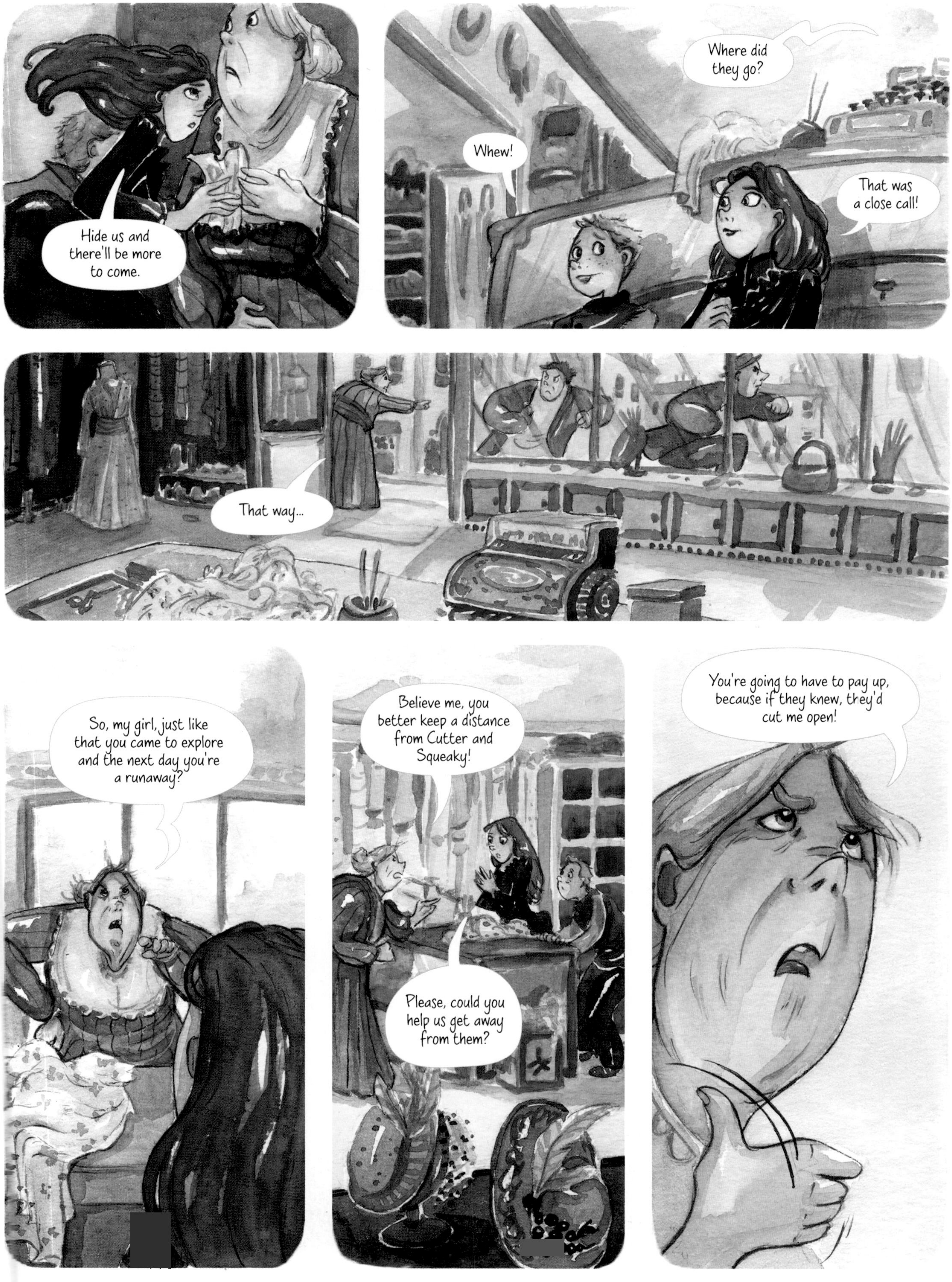
Hide us and there'll be more to come.
Where did they go?
Whew!
That was a close call!
That way...
So, my girl, just like that you came to explore and the next day you're a runaway?
Believe me, you better keep a distance from Cutter and Squeaky!
Please, could you help us get away from them?
You're going to have to pay up, because if they knew, they'd cut me open!

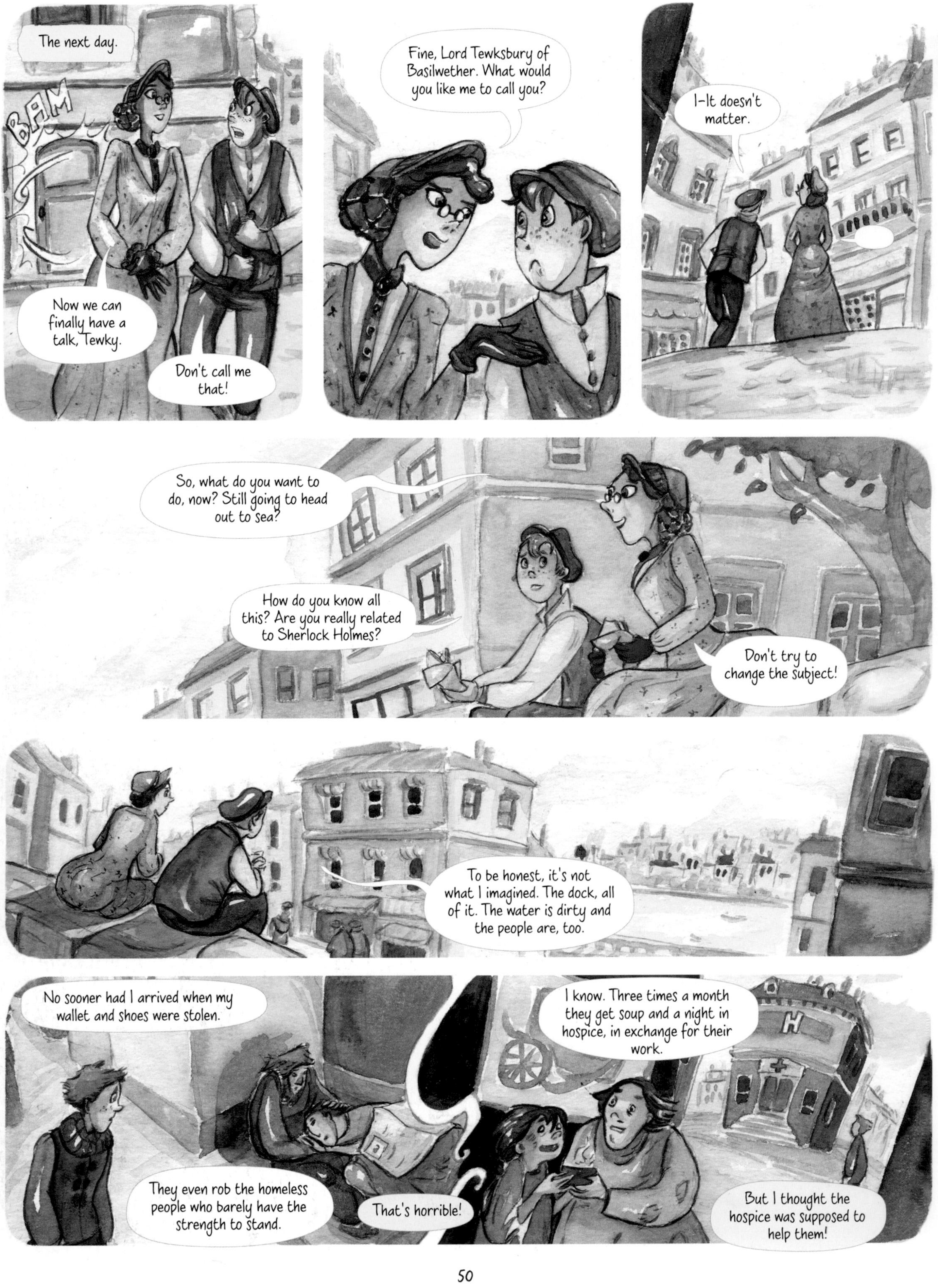
The next day.
BAM
Now we can finally have a talk, Tewky.
Don't call me that!
Fine, Lord Tewksbury of Basilwether. What would you like me to call you?
I-It doesn't matter.
So, what do you want to do, now? Still going to head out to sea?
How do you know all this? Are you really related to Sherlock Holmes?
Don't try to change the subject!
To be honest, it's not what I imagined. The dock, all of it. The water is dirty and the people are, too.
No sooner had I arrived when my wallet and shoes were stolen.
They even rob the homeless people who barely have the strength to stand.
That's horrible!
I know. Three times a month they get soup and a night in hospice, in exchange for their work.
But I thought the hospice was supposed to help them!
H

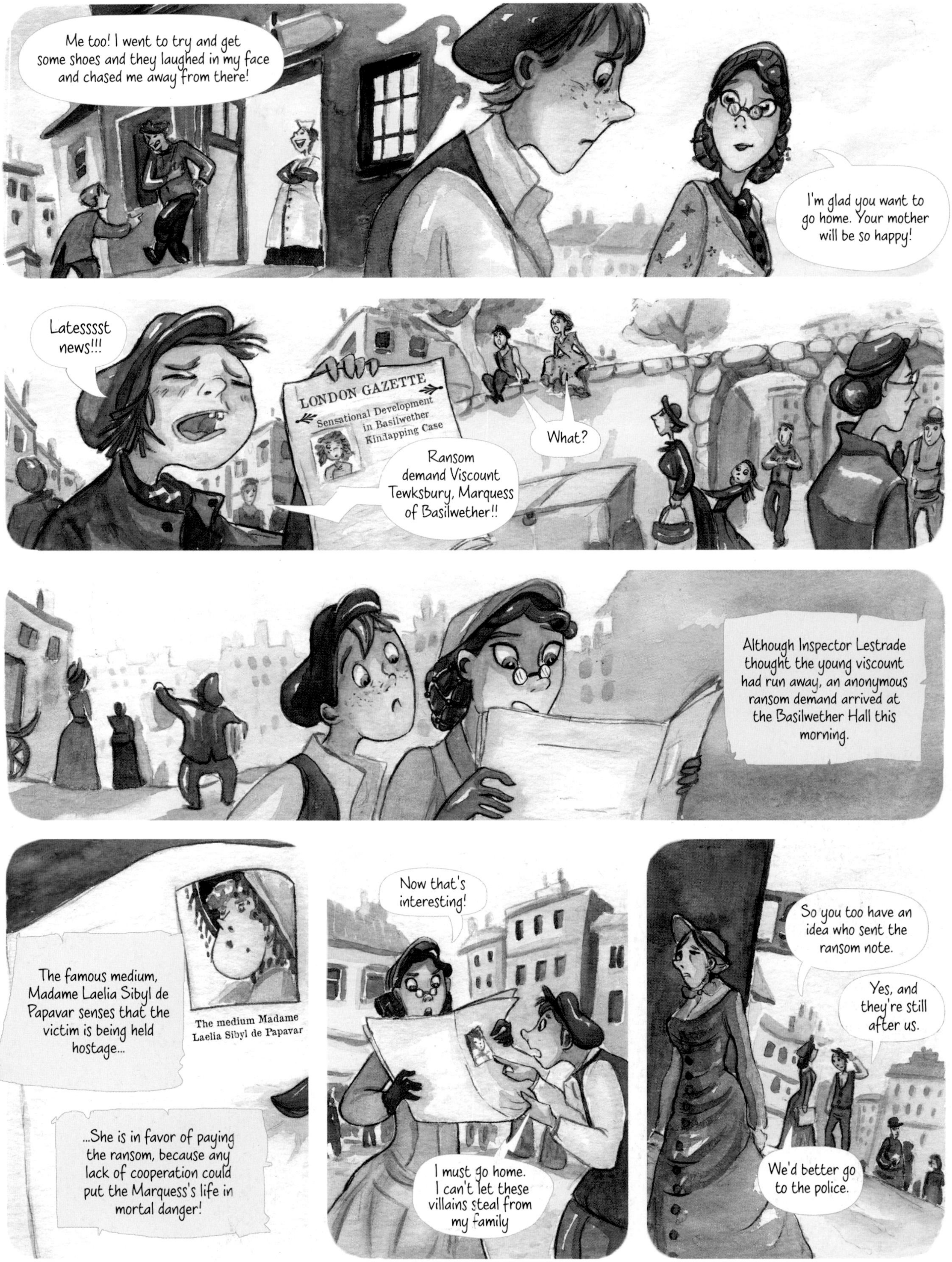
Me too! I went to try and get some shoes and they laughed in my face and chased me away from there!
I'm glad you want to go home. Your mother will be so happy!
Latesssst news!!!
LONDON GAZETTE
Sensational Development in Basilwether Kindapping Case
What?
Ransom demand Viscount Tewksbury, Marquess of Basilwether!!
Although Inspector Lestrade thought the young viscount had run away, an anonymous ransom demand arrived at the Basilwether Hall this morning.
The famous medium, Madame Laelia Sibyl de Papavar senses that the victim is being held hostage...
The medium Madame Laelia Sibyl de Papavar
...She is in favor of paying the ransom, because any lack of cooperation could put the Marquess's life in mortal danger!
Now that's interesting!
I must go home. I can't let these villains steal from my family
So you too have an idea who sent the ransom note.
Yes, and they're still after us.
We'd better go to the police.

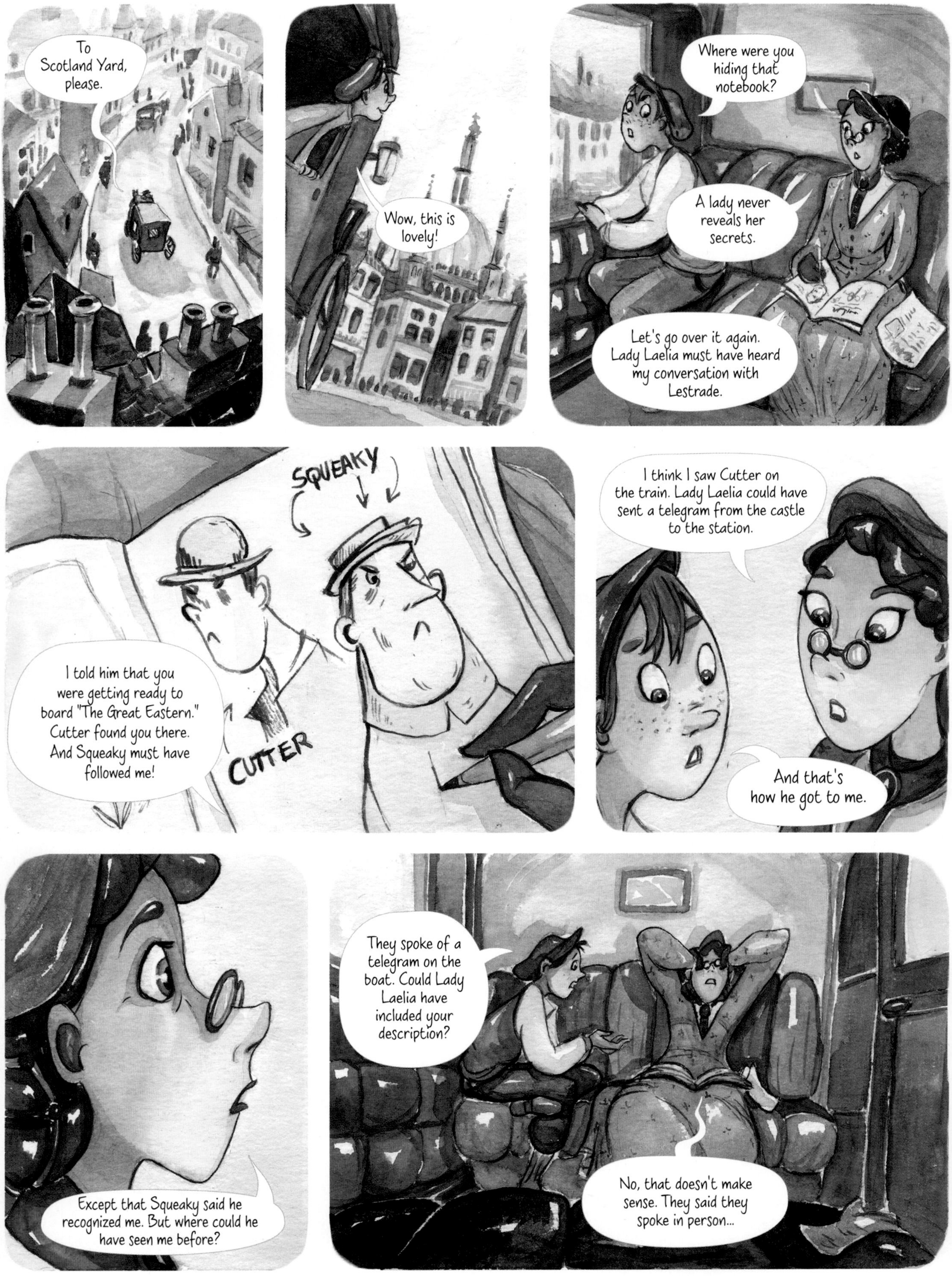
To Scotland Yard, please.
Wow, this is lovely!
Where were you hiding that notebook?
A lady never reveals her secrets.
Let's go over it again. Lady Laelia must have heard my conversation with Lestrade.
SQUEAKY
CUTTER
I told him that you were getting ready to board "The Great Eastern." Cutter found you there. And Squeaky must have followed me!
I think I saw Cutter on the train. Lady Laelia could have sent a telegram from the castle to the station.
And that's how he got to me.
Except that Squeaky said he recognized me. But where could he have seen me before?
They spoke of a telegram on the boat. Could Lady Laelia have included your description?
No, that doesn't make sense. They said they spoke in person...

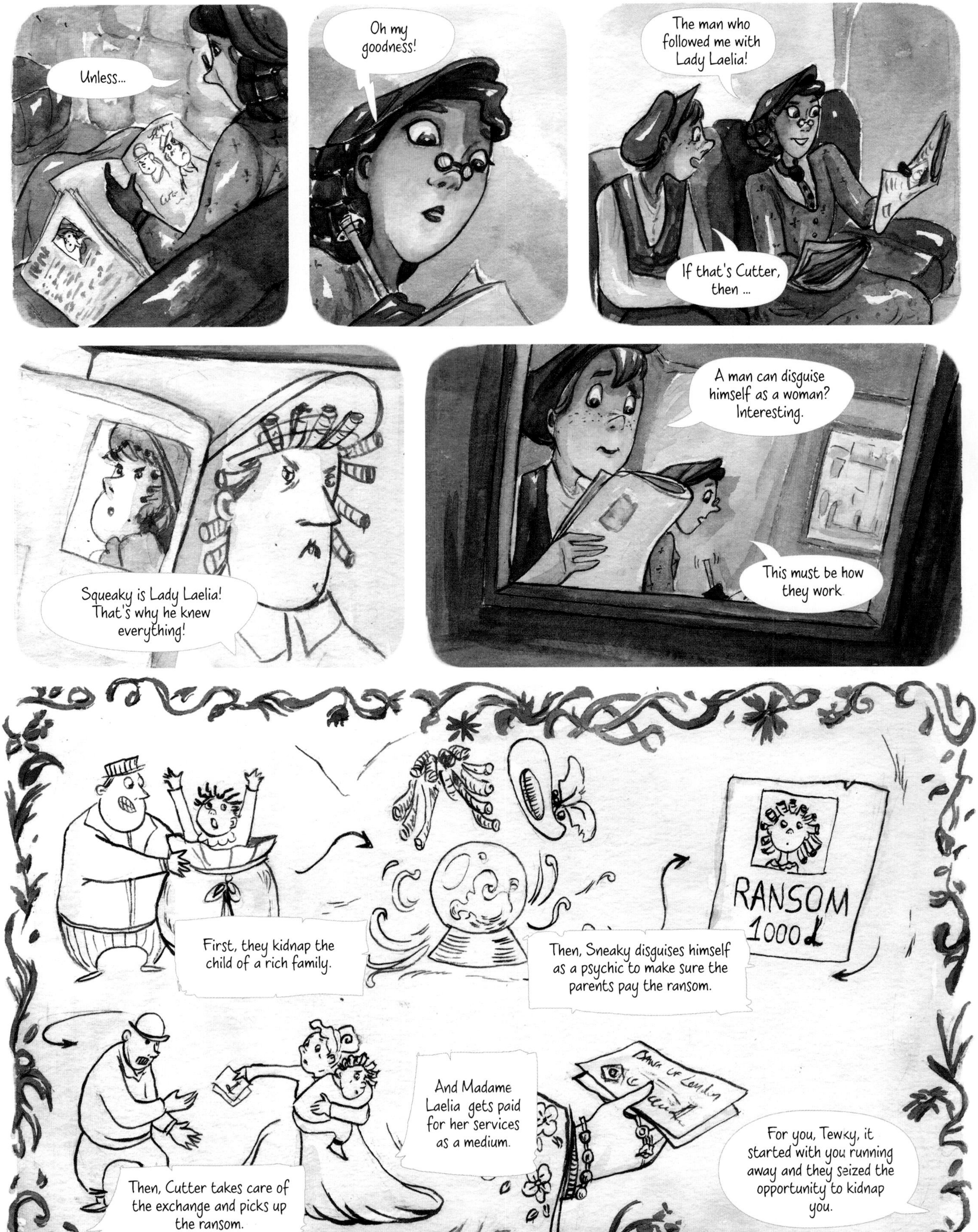

Unless...
Oh my goodness!
The man who followed me with Lady Laelia!
If that's Cutter, then ...
Squeaky is Lady Laelia! That's why he knew everything!
A man can disguise himself as a woman? Interesting.
This must be how they work.
First, they kidnap the child of a rich family.
Then, Sneaky disguises himself as a psychic to make sure the parents pay the ransom.
RANSOM 1000 £
Then, Cutter takes care of the exchange and picks up the ransom.
And Madame Laelia gets paid for her services as a medium.
For you, Tewky, it started with you running away and they seized the opportunity to kidnap you.

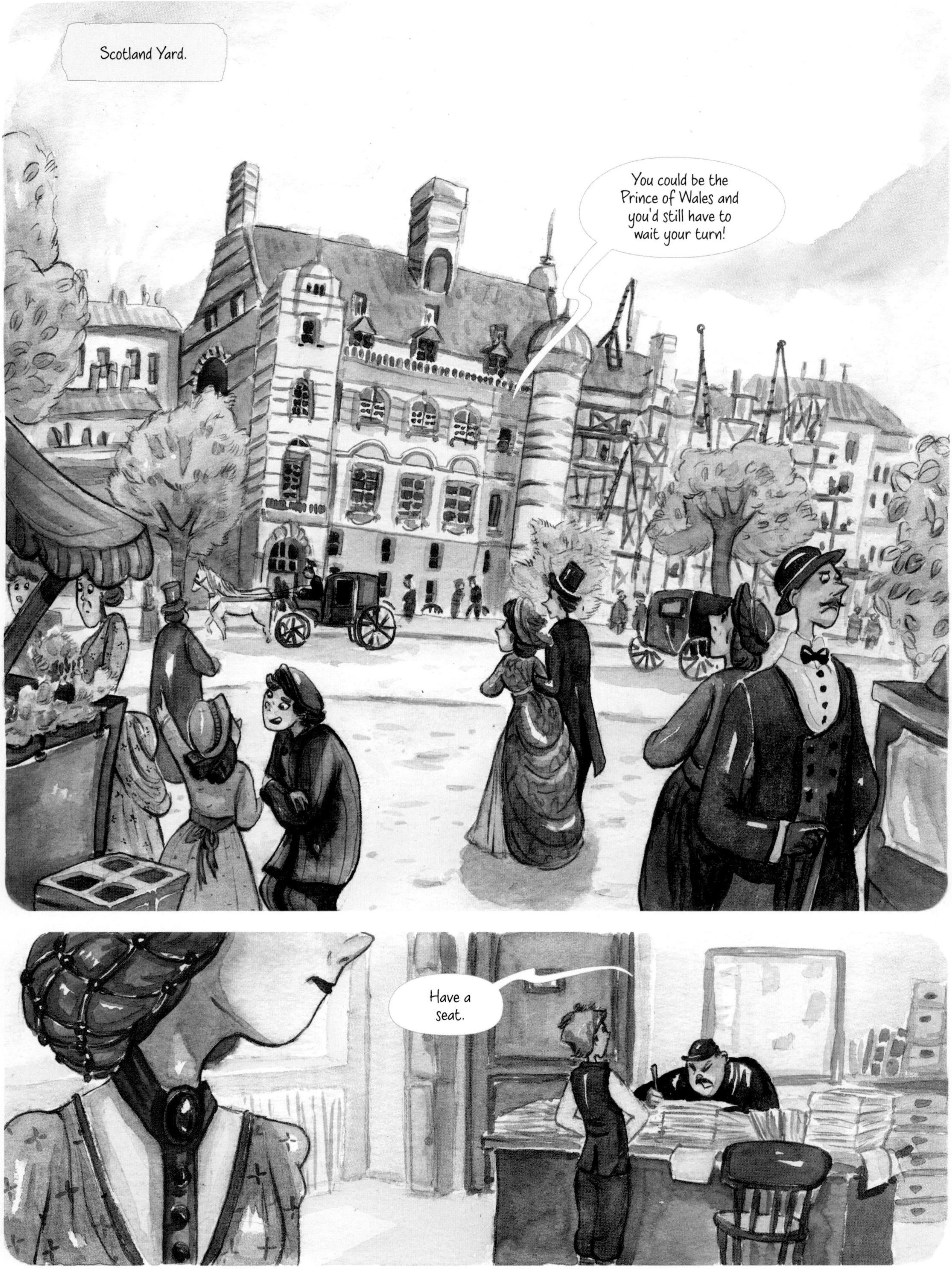
Scotland Yard.
You could be the Prince of Wales and you'd still have to wait your turn!
Have a seat.

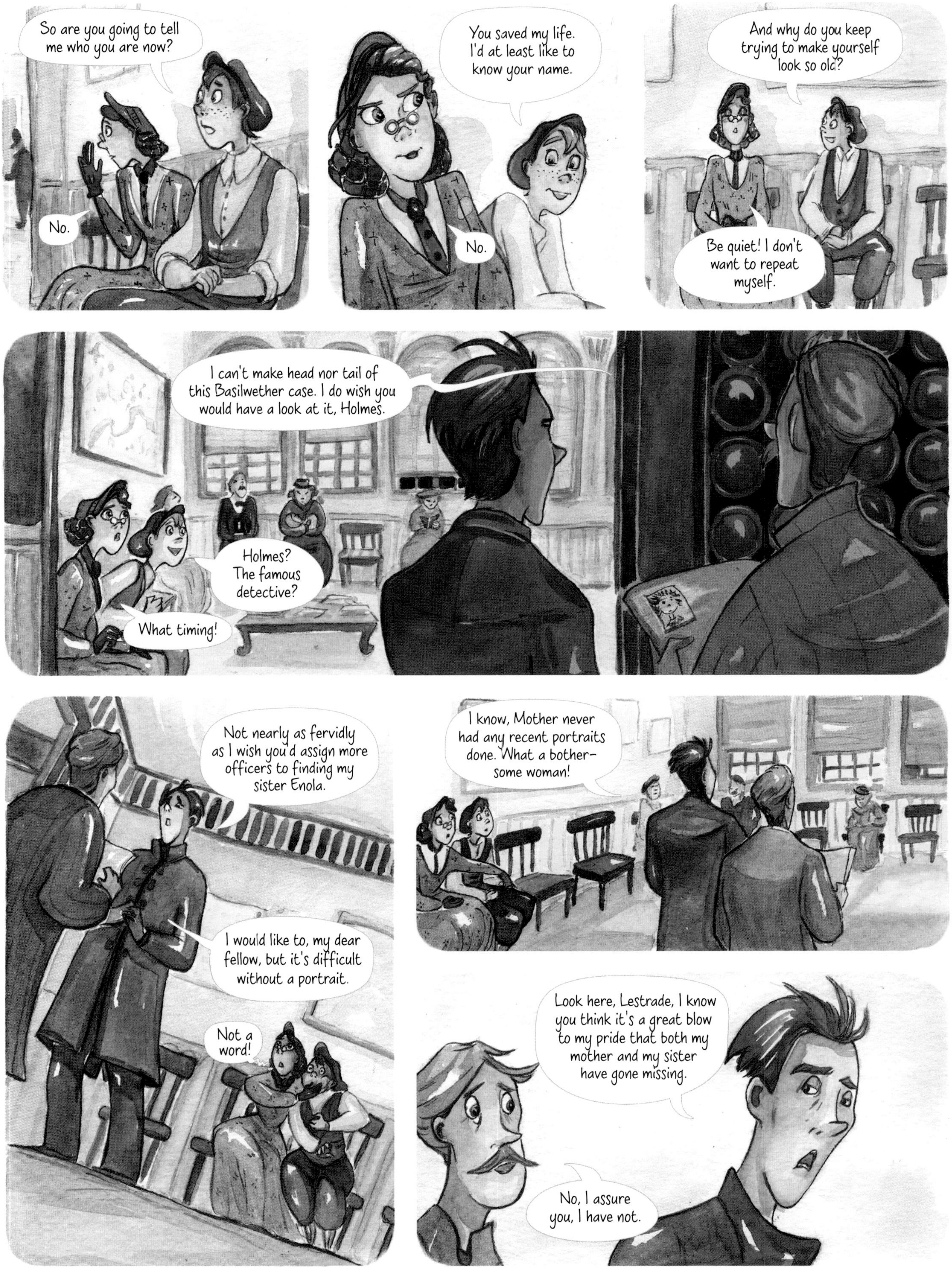

So are you going to tell me who you are now?
No.
You saved my life. I'd at least like to know your name.
No.
And why do you keep trying to make yourself look so old?
Be quiet! I don't want to repeat myself.
I can't make head nor tail of this Basilwether case. I do wish you would have a look at it, Holmes.
Holmes? The famous detective?
What timing!
Not nearly as fervidly as I wish you'd assign more officers to finding my sister Enola.
I would like to, my dear fellow, but it's difficult without a portrait.
Not a word!
I know, Mother never had any recent portraits done. What a bother-some woman!
Look here, Lestrade, I know you think it's a great blow to my pride that both my mother and my sister have gone missing.
No, I assure you, I have not.

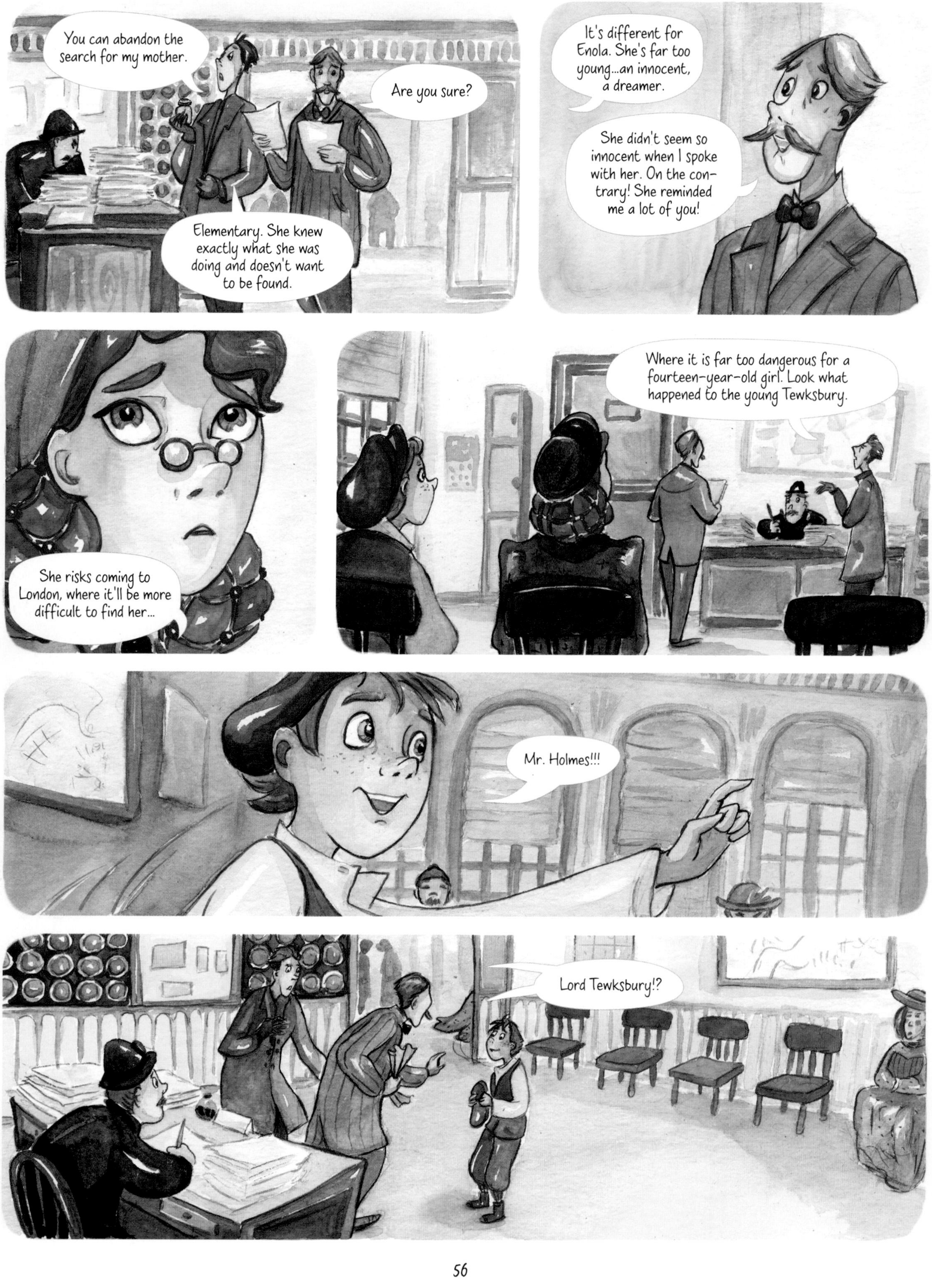
You can abandon the search for my mother.
Are you sure?
Elementary. She knew exactly what she was doing and doesn't want to be found.
It's different for Enola. She's far too young...an innocent, a dreamer.
She didn't seem so innocent when I spoke with her. On the contrary! She reminded me a lot of you!
She risks coming to London, where it'll be more difficult to find her...
Where it is far too dangerous for a fourteen-year-old girl. Look what happened to the young Tewksbury.
Mr. Holmes!!!
Lord Tewksbury!?

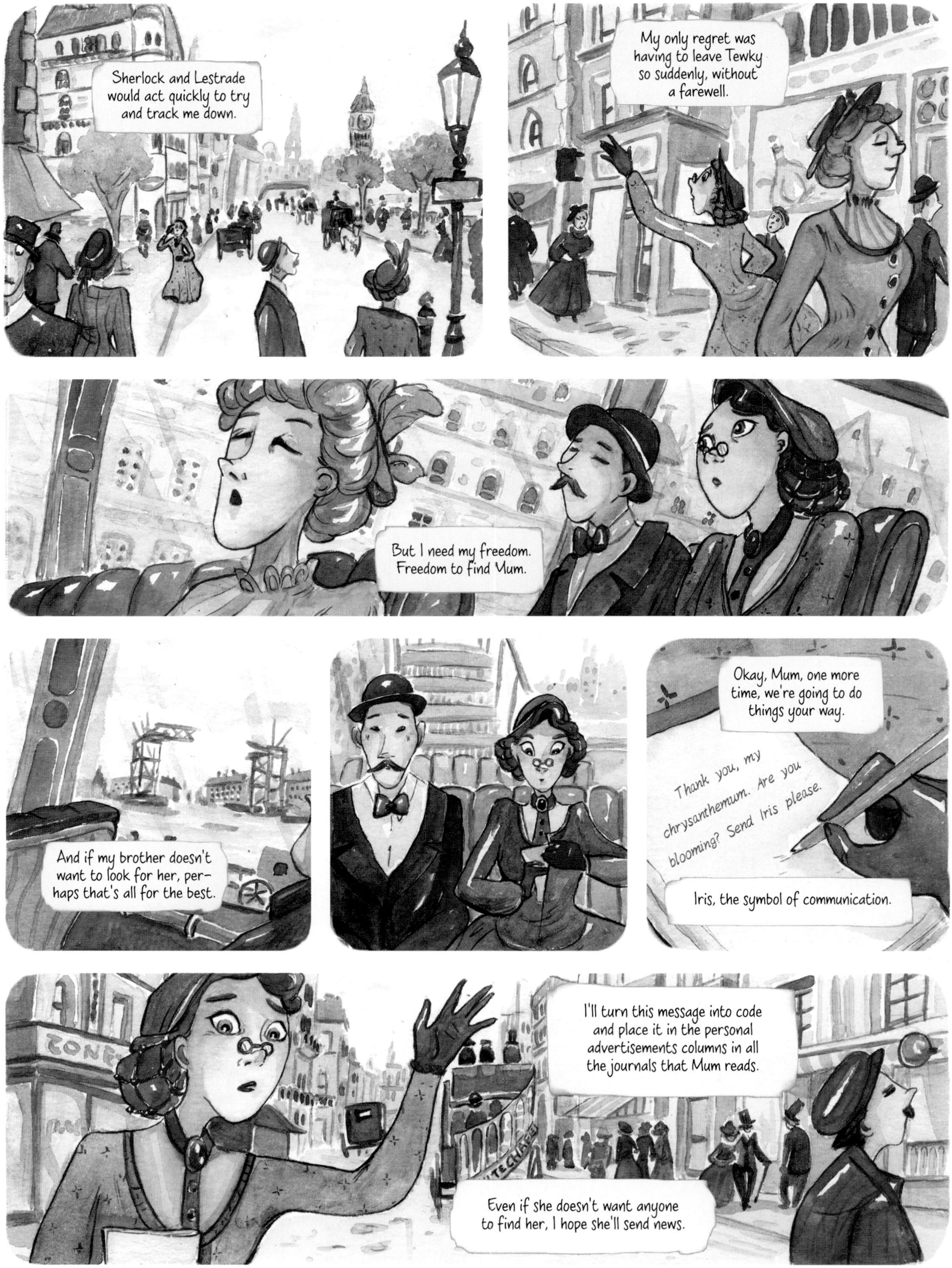
Sherlock and Lestrade would act quickly to try and track me down.
My only regret was having to leave Tewky so suddenly, without a farewell.
But I need my freedom. Freedom to find Mum.
And if my brother doesn't want to look for her, perhaps that's all for the best.
Okay, Mum, one more time, we're going to do things your way.
Thank you, my chrysanthemum. Are you blooming? Send Iris please.
Iris, the symbol of communication.
I'll turn this message into code and place it in the personal advertisements columns in all the journals that Mum reads.
Even if she doesn't want anyone to find her, I hope she'll send news.

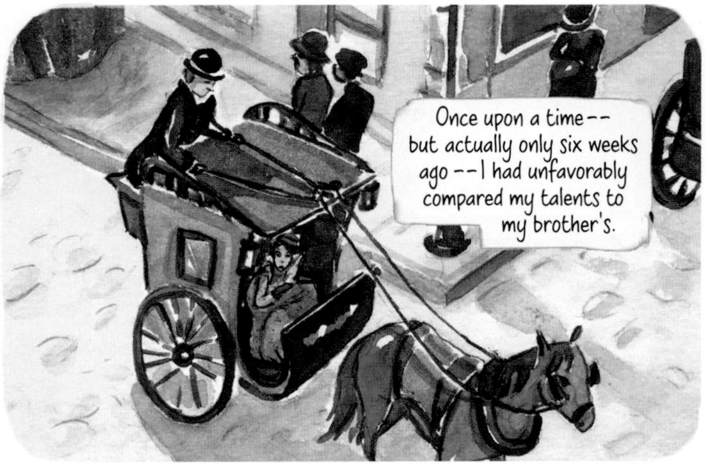
Once upon a time-- but actually only six weeks ago --I had unfavorably compared my talents to my brother's.

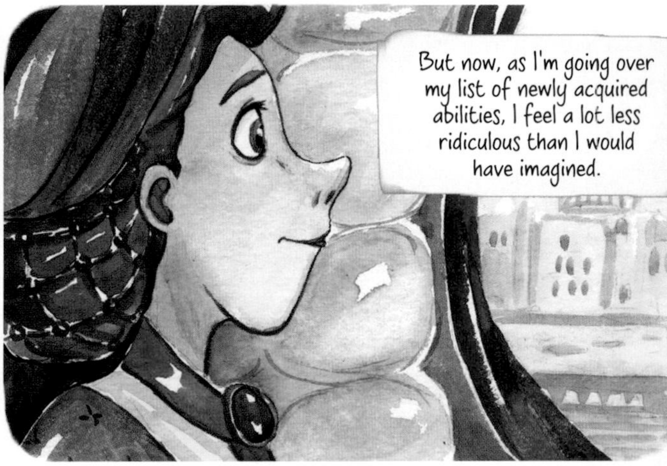
But now, as I'm going over my list of newly acquired abilities, I feel a lot less ridiculous than I would have imagined.

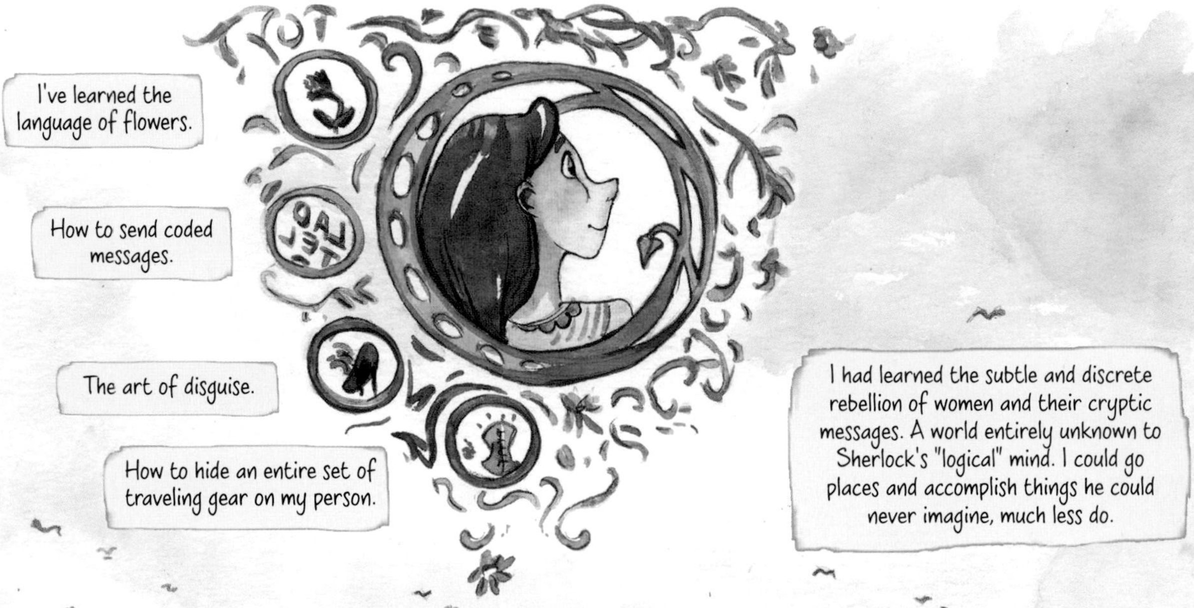
I've learned the language of flowers.
How to send coded messages.
The art of disguise.
How to hide an entire set of traveling gear on my person.
I had learned the subtle and discrete rebellion of women and their cryptic messages. A world entirely unknown to Sherlock's "logical" mind. I could go places and accomplish things he could never imagine, much less do.

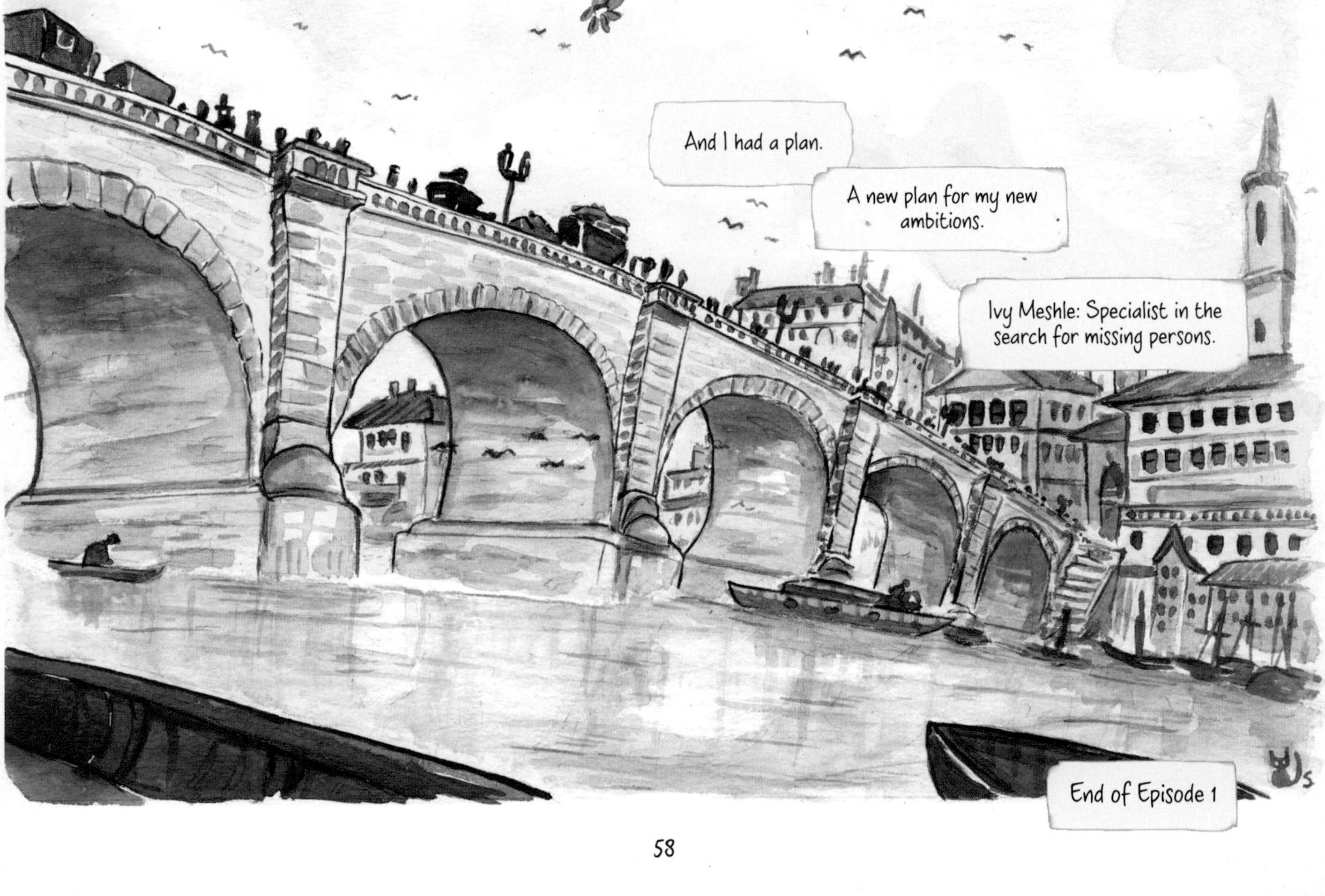
And I had a plan.
A new plan for my new ambitions.
Ivy Meshle: Specialist in the search for missing persons.
End of Episode 1

SECRET NOTEBOOK

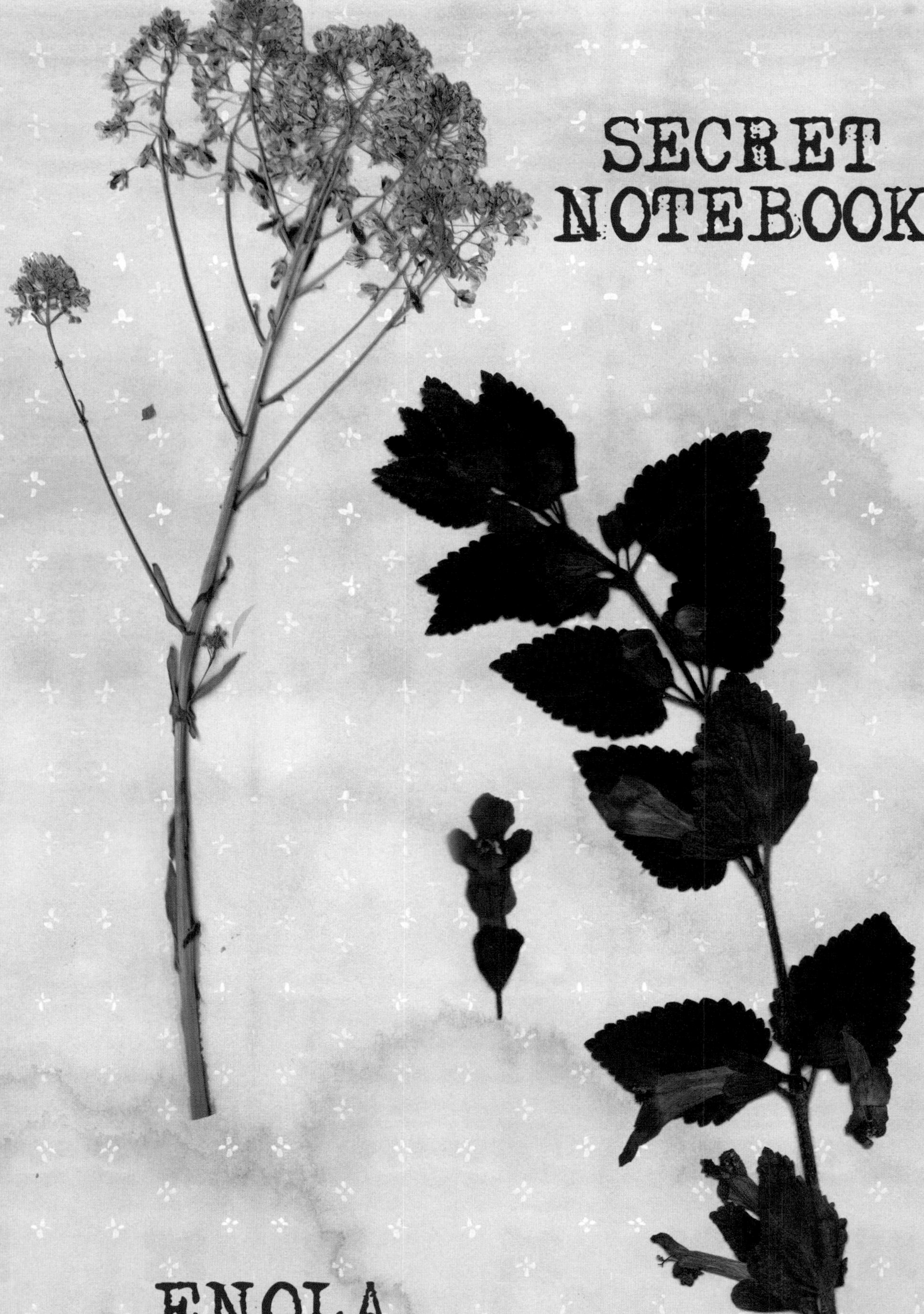

ENOLA HOLMES

The Language of Flowers

Ivy :
Fidelity.
To become attached.

Thistle :
Defiance.

Sweetpea :
Good-bye and thank you for a lovely
time. A gift given upon departure.

Iris :
I'm sending you a message.
I know how to prove my love.

Chamomile :
Strength in adversity.
I follow you very closely.

Rambling Rose :
Symbol of a free life as
a vagabond.

Rhododendron :
Danger is near, be careful.

Violet :
In all modesty.

Chrysanthemum :
Familial attachment and, by
implication, affection.

Primrose :
I wish you eternal youth.

Lily of the Valley :
Happiness, found at last.

Bear's Ear :
Don't ask me anything!

Lettuce :
I won't abandon you.

Poppy :
I see your sadness.
Let me comfort you.

Daisy :
Symbol of innocence.

Narcissus :
You only love yourself.
Egotist.

Pansy :
I need attention.

Blue Sage :
I'm thinking of you.

Rockfoil :
With all my heart.

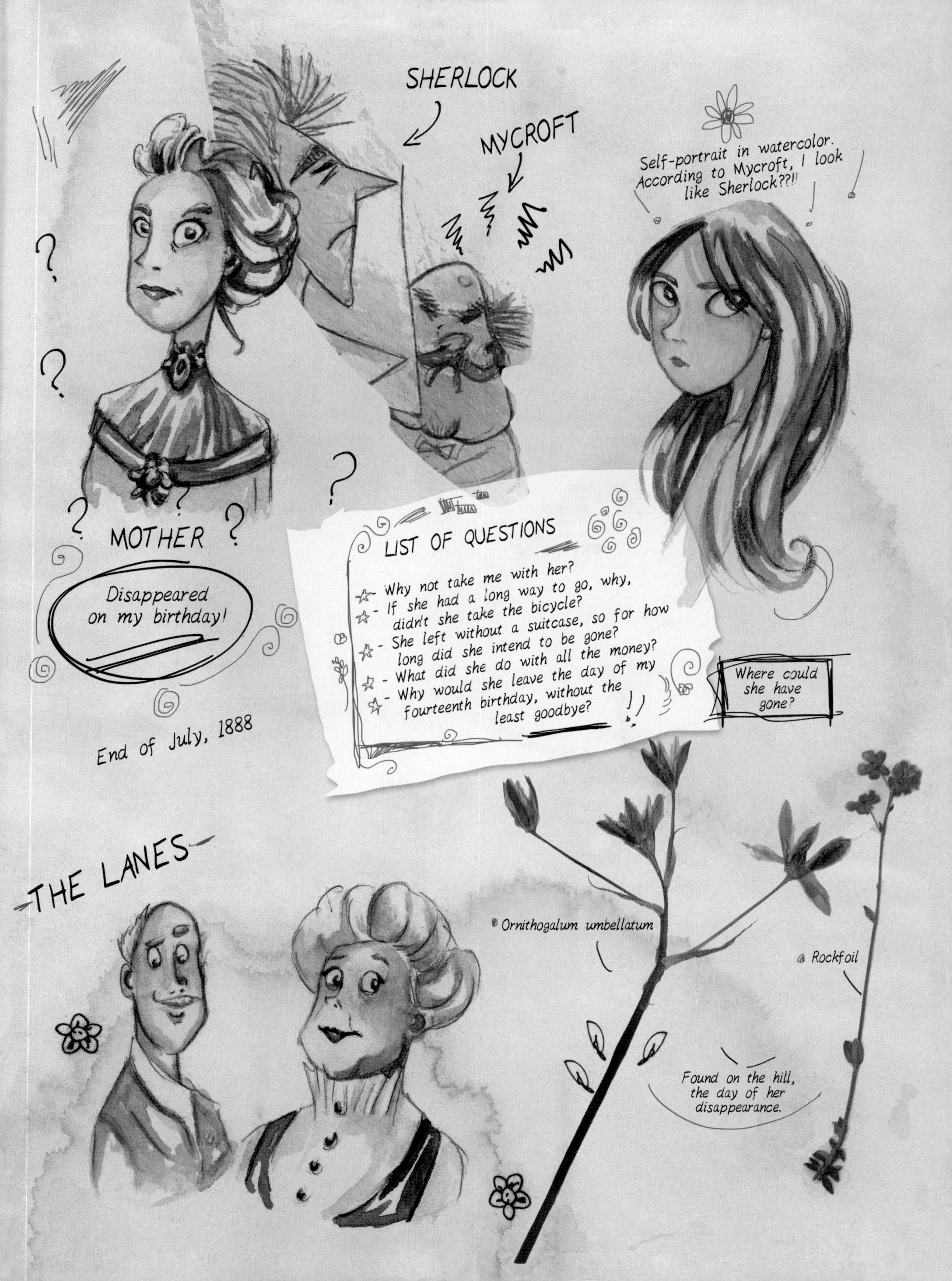
SHERLOCK
MYCROFT
Self-portrait in watercolor. According to Mycroft, I look like Sherlock??!!
MOTHER
Disappeared on my birthday!
End of July, 1888
LIST OF QUESTIONS
- Why not take me with her?
- If she had a long way to go, why, didn't she take the bicycle?
- She left without a suitcase, so for how long did she intend to be gone?
- What did she do with all the money?
- Why would she leave the day of my fourteenth birthday, without the least goodbye?
Where could she have gone?
THE LANES
Ornithogalum umbellatum
Rockfoil
Found on the hill, the day of her disappearance.

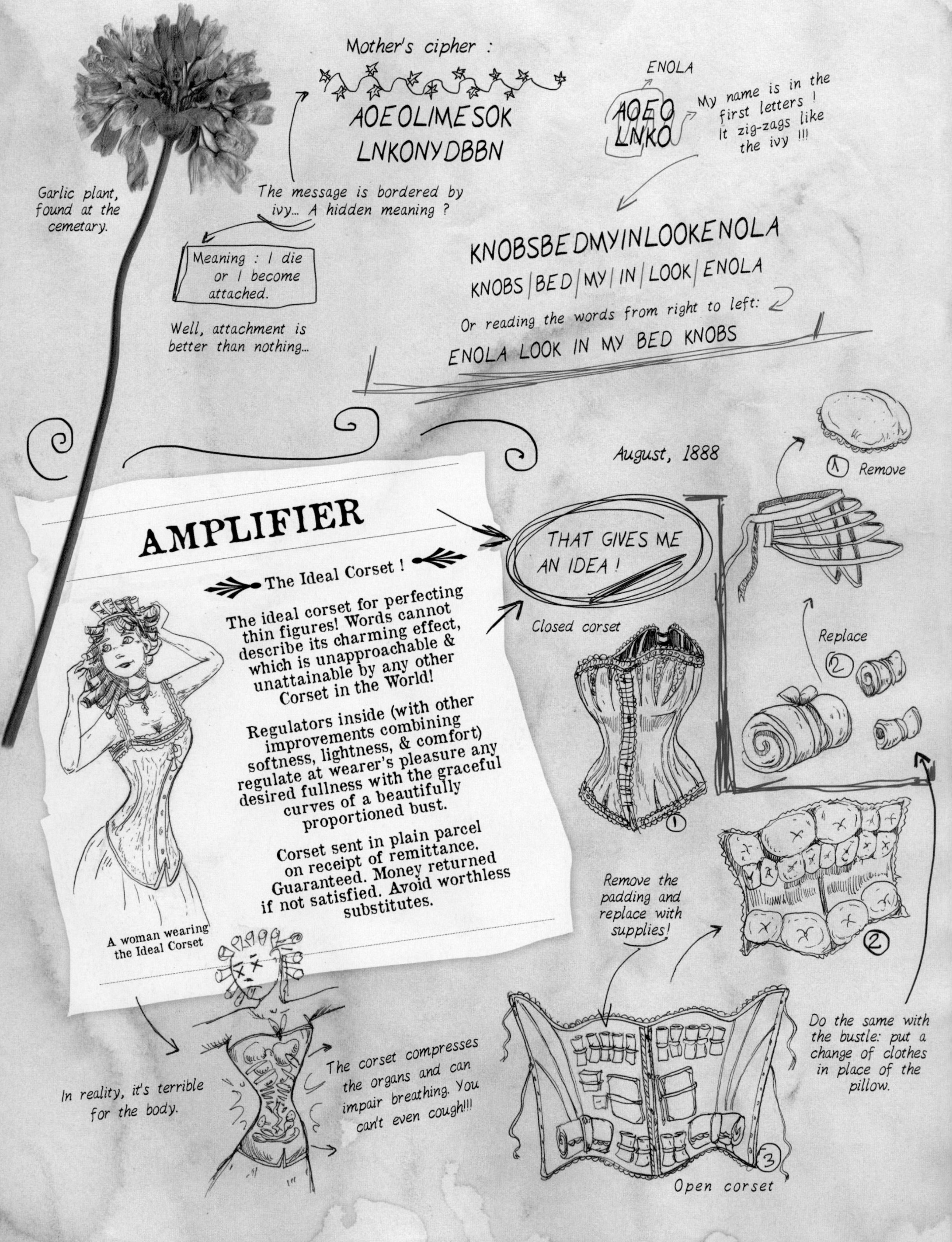
Mother's cipher :
AOEOLIMESOK
LNKONYDBBN
The message is bordered by ivy... A hidden meaning ?
Garlic plant, found at the cemetary.
Meaning : I die or I become attached.
Well, attachment is better than nothing...
ENOLA
AOEO
LNKO
My name is in the first letters ! It zig-zags like the ivy !!!
KNOBSBEDMYINLOOKENOLA
KNOBS | BED | MY | IN | LOOK | ENOLA
Or reading the words from right to left:
ENOLA LOOK IN MY BED KNOBS
August, 1888
AMPLIFIER
The Ideal Corset !
The ideal corset for perfecting thin figures! Words cannot describe its charming effect, which is unapproachable & unattainable by any other Corset in the World!
Regulators inside (with other improvements combining softness, lightness, & comfort) regulate at wearer's pleasure any desired fullness with the graceful curves of a beautifully proportioned bust.
Corset sent in plain parcel on receipt of remittance. Guaranteed. Money returned if not satisfied. Avoid worthless substitutes.
A woman wearing the Ideal Corset
THAT GIVES ME AN IDEA !
Closed corset
1 Remove
Replace
2
1
2
Remove the padding and replace with supplies!
In reality, it's terrible for the body.
The corset compresses the organs and can impair breathing. You can't even cough!!!
Do the same with the bustle: put a change of clothes in place of the pillow.
3
Open corset

September, 1888

THE KIDNAPPED HEIR!

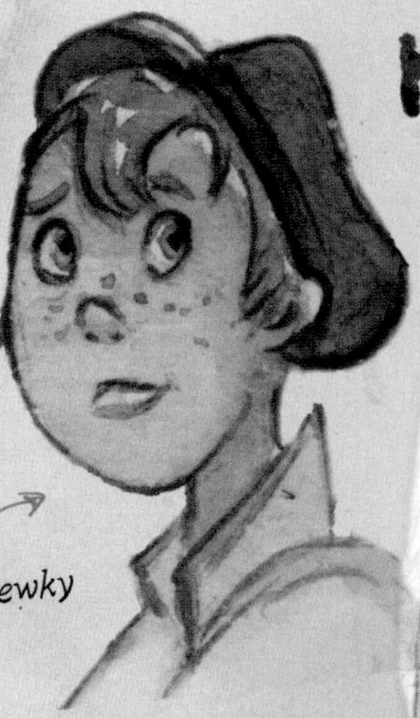
Tewky

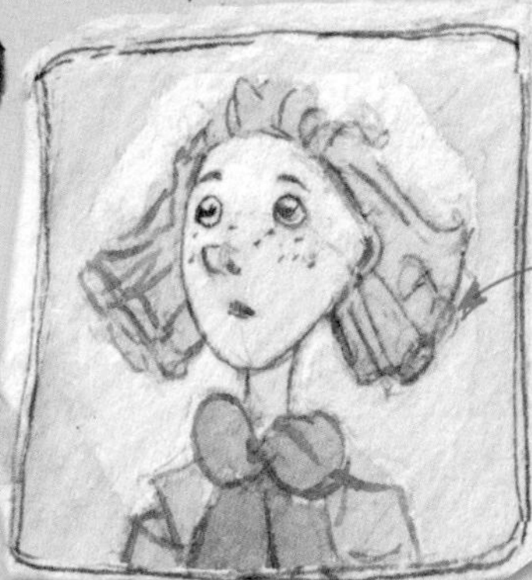

Article summarizing the facts:

Early in the morning a gardener at Basilwether Hall noticed that the French window to the billiard room was forced open. Fearful of burglary, the butler checked the silver and other valuable contents of the drawing room and discovered nothing was missing.

The household staff was alerted. It was a housemaid who discovered that something had become of the young viscount of Tewksbury, a boy just twelve years old. The young viscount's furnishings were strewn about the room, evidence of a desperate struggle, and of his noble personage there was no sign...

A little melodramatic!

List made last night when I couldn't sleep.

- Why did Cutter think I knew where to find Tewky ?
- What does he want with Tewky ?
- Is he a professional kidnapper ?
- How did he know about the Great Eastern ?

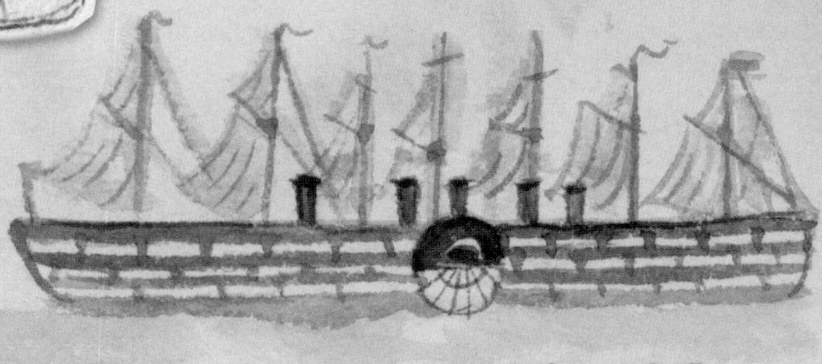

THE GREAT EASTERN

Article about the ransom demand !!!

Though Inspector Lestrade thought the young viscount had run away, an anonymous ransom demand arrived at the Basilwether Hall this morning.

The Spiritualist Medium Madame Laiela Sybil de Papavar senses that the victim is being held hostage and is in favor of the ransom, because any lack of cooperation would put him in danger of dying !

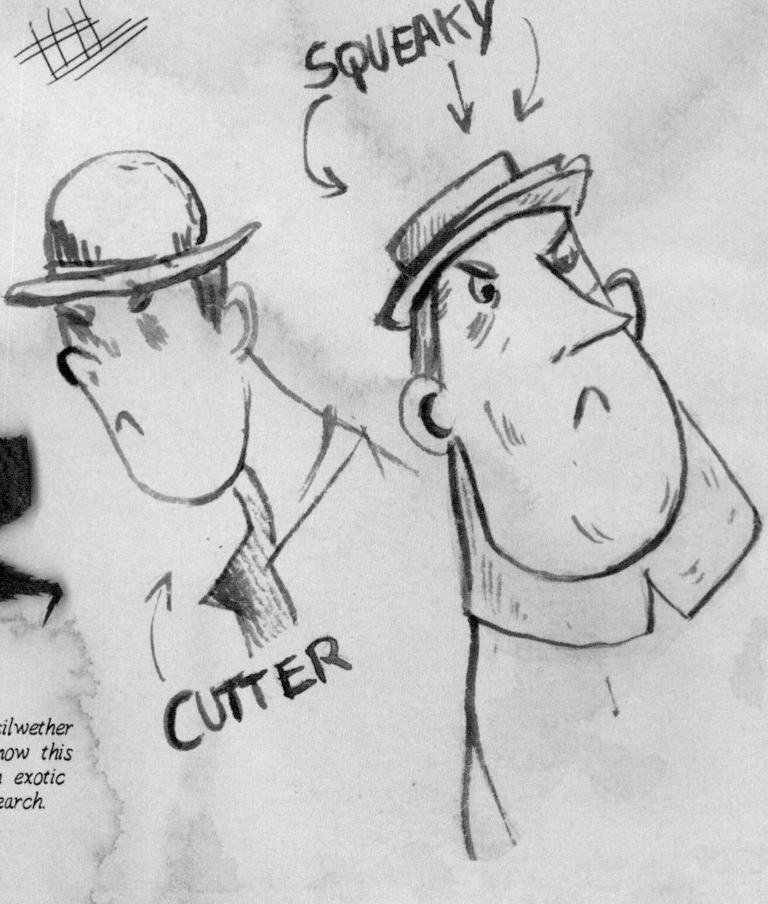
SQUEAKY
CUTTER

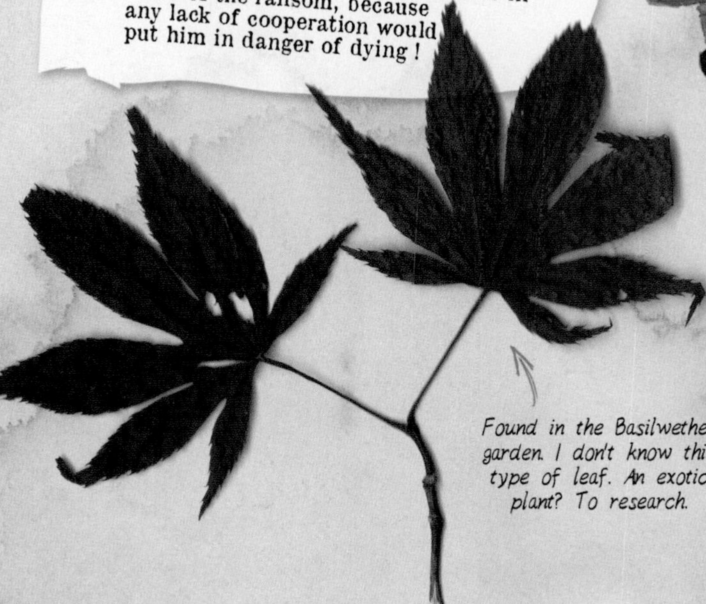

Found in the Basilwether garden. I don't know this type of leaf. An exotic plant? To research.

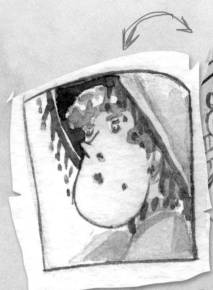

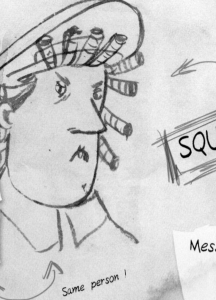

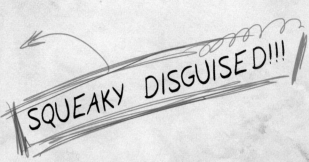

SQUEAKY DISGUISED!!!

Portrait of the medium found in the journal.

Same person !

Message to encode for Mother :

THANK YOU, MY CHRYSANTHEMUM. ARE YOU BLOOMING ? SEND IRIS PLEASE.

CREATE A SECRET CODE

Taking the message I composed, I reversed it:

ESAELPSIRIDNES?GNIMOOLBUOYERAM
UMEHTNASYRHCYMUOYKNAHT

And rewrote in zig-zag:

EALSRDE?NMOBOEAUETAYHYUYNH
SEPIINSGIOLUYRMMHNSRCMOKAT

My message would look like this in the journal:

Tails ivy SEPIINSGIOLUYRMMHNSRCMOKAT
tips ivy ALSRDE?NMOBOEAUE-TAYHYUYNH
your Ivy

November, 1888

Mother answered !!!
Reply to the message foundin the journal !

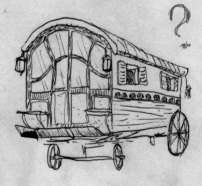

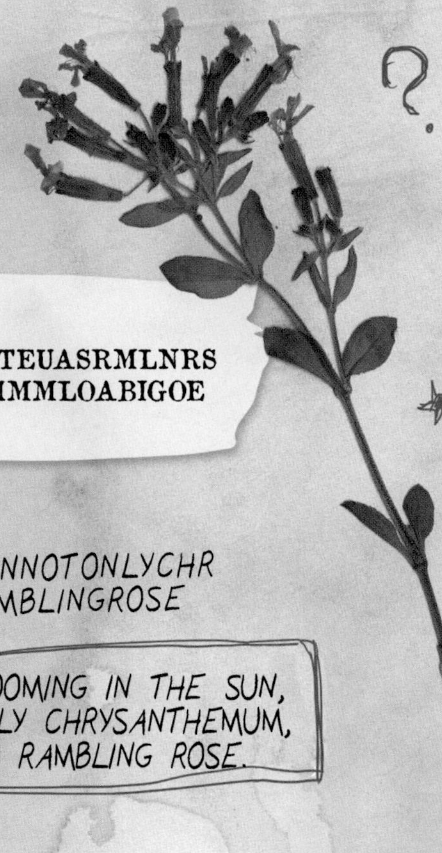

Iris tipstails to Ivy
ABOMNITEUNTNYHYATEUASRMLNRS
MLOIGNHSNOOLCRSNHMMLOABIGOE

Follow the zig-zags again.

AMBLOOMINGINTHESUNNOTONLYCHR
YSANTHEMUMALSORAMBLINGROSE

AM BLOOMING IN THE SUN, NOT ONLY CHRYSANTHEMUM, ALSO RAMBLING ROSE.

New list of questions about Mother :

- If she had a long way to go, why didn't she take the bicycle ?
- Why didn't she leave through the big gate ?
- Where was she going ?
- If she also planned my escape, why not just take me with her ?

TO BE CONTINUED ---